P9-CQG-828

Read the wonderful reviews for RITA® Award-winning author Helen Brenna

Dear Reader,

Unbeknownst to me, the seeds for this story were planted during the lazy days of summer family vacations and have been growing in my heart for years.

A long time ago we visited nothing less than a fairyland in the midst of reality—Mackinac Island, Michigan. My daughter claims she had one of the best days of her life horseback riding, eating homemade fudge and enjoying her first-ever carriage ride. Then there were the camping and fishing trips to Wisconsin, my home away from home. We've traveled up and down that state, but I have wonderful memories of our excursions to the Apostle Islands.

So what do you get when you cross Mackinac with an Apostle Island? That'd be Mirabelle, a quaint, idyllic village surrounded by rustic wilderness. What makes Mirabelle Island particularly special, though, are the characters. They're loyal, quirky and lovable, some more than others. These islanders, especially Noah and Sophie, came alive for me. I hope they do for you, too!

I loved Mirabelle so much I couldn't get enough of the place. Keep an eye out for *Next Comes Love* and *Then Comes Baby,* two more stories set on Mirabelle, coming in October and December 2009.

Happy reading!

Helen Brenna

FIRST COME TWINS
Helen Brenna

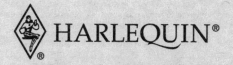

TORONTO • NEW YORK • LONDON
AMSTERDAM • PARIS • SYDNEY • HAMBURG
STOCKHOLM • ATHENS • TOKYO • MILAN • MADRID
PRAGUE • WARSAW • BUDAPEST • AUCKLAND

Recycling programs
for this product may
not exist in your area.

ISBN-13: 978-0-373-71582-4

FIRST COME TWINS

Copyright © 2009 by Helen Brenna.

www.eHarlequin.com

Printed in U.S.A.

ABOUT THE AUTHOR

Helen Brenna grew up in a small town in central Minnesota, the seventh of eight children. Although she never dreamed of writing books, she's always been a voracious reader of romances. So after taking a break from her accounting career, she tried her hand at writing the romances she loves to read. Since her first book was published in 2007, she's not only won the Romance Writers of America's prestigious RITA® Award and Virginia Romance Writers' Holt Medallion, she's also been nominated several times for *Romantic Times BOOKreviews* Reviewers' Choice awards.

Helen still lives in Minnesota with her husband, two children and too many pets. She'd love hearing from you. E-mail her at helenbrenna@comcast.net or send mail to P.O. Box 24107, Minneapolis, MN 55424. Visit her Web site at www.helenbrenna.com or chat with Helen and other authors at RidingWithTheTopDown.blogspot.com.

Books by Helen Brenna

HARLEQUIN SUPERROMANCE
1403—TREASURE
1425—DAD FOR LIFE
1519—FINDING MR. RIGHT

HARLEQUIN NASCAR
PEAK PERFORMANCE

For Joan Ulrich Twomey

The strongest, most resilient and compassionate woman I know and I get to call her Mom!

Acknowledgments

The real hero of this book is Adam Gadach. Several years ago Adam lost his leg in a car accident after being hit by a drunk driver. His determination and willingness to share his struggles regarding his injuries and life with a prosthetic deeply touched me. If Noah Bennett depicts even a portion of Adam's courage, then I've done my job well.

I'd also like to thank Teresa Gadach, Adam's aunt, for her suggestions relating to this book, but mostly for her friendship and encouragement through these many, many years. Love you!

A shout-out to Michelle Schmidt for sharing with me her extensive knowledge of photography. And thanks for making plain-Jane me feel like a princess for a day.

CHAPTER ONE

"WHAT A QUAINT LITTLE ISLAND."

"This place is gorgeous."

"Look at all the flowers."

Hanging toward the back of the throng of tourists, Noah Bennett only half listened to their jabbering as they filed off the Mirabelle Island ferry and onto the pier. The idiots couldn't wait to get off the boat before snapping pictures left and right.

"Oh, get that storefront. And the lamppost."

A lamppost. That one's sure to win a Pulitzer.

"I already love this place."

"It's so charming."

Yeah. And boring. And quiet. With nosy neighbors and absolutely nothing to do. You should all love it.

Hell, man, chill.

Taking in a deep breath, Noah did his best to dispel the anger that seemed to be his constant companion these days and tried to be patient while the last of the tourists exited the boat deck. They were all in so much of a hurry, and with his bum leg he'd only slow everyone up. He'd put this off for a decade and a half, five more minutes weren't going to kill him. It's not as if there'd be a welcoming committee waiting.

As the ferry cleared out, he couldn't help noticing there weren't any families. The majority of people heading down the pier were couples, both young and old. That was strange. Although it was only the end of May, used to be, this place was crawling with kids. Still, they all were happy people, all on vacation, all ready for an idyllic few days. They'd find it. Mirabelle was that kind of place for most folks.

After asking one of the attendants to have his luggage delivered to Grandma Bennett's house, Noah adjusted his baseball cap and sunglasses, hoping to maintain his anonymity for a few days, and made his way off the ferry. By the time he left the pier his temporary prosthetic felt like a lead weight at the end of what was left of his leg.

They'd said he'd be good as new. *Right.* On what planet? He forced himself to walk to the end of the block before dropping onto the bench at the curb, not far from where the ferry passengers were catching carriage rides to their respective accommodations.

A look down Main Street took his mind off the dull ache in his leg. Other than the oak trees, maples, lindens and spruce being noticeably larger, little had changed on this chunk of dirt since the day he'd left. Miller's Ice Creamery and Candy Shoppe was still painted fire-engine red with white shutters, though they now offered gourmet coffees. There was a sedate new art gallery and two new restaurant-bar combos, although Duffy's Pub looked as entrenched as before. The bank, post office, floral shop and village chapel all looked exactly the same, from the green-and-white striped awnings to the baskets of flowers hanging from the black iron lampposts.

That's the way they liked it here on Mirabelle. Newfangled was bad. Static was good. Retro was better. And historic, well, now you were cooking with gas.

What had he been thinking coming back here? With nothing but a village on one end of the long and narrow island, a couple of isolated private homes on the other, and undeveloped state land sandwiched in between, he'd hated Mirabelle. Every minute of every day after hitting adolescence had been torture for Noah. Sophie had been the only reason he'd remained on the island past his sixteenth birthday. How ironic that after he'd left, she'd been the reason he'd stayed away. Well, her and Isaac, anyway.

Noah dreaded seeing his brother again after all these years. Every few minutes, he wavered between wanting to punch Isaac for what he'd done or hug the daylights out of him for missing him. Maybe Noah should've gone to his beach house in Rhode Island. Though he hadn't spent enough time there through the years for it to truly feel like a home, it might've been peaceful enough for what the doctors had in mind.

The ferry horn tooted, catching him off guard, and the explosion burst front and center in his mind. The rumble, like a small earthquake. The smells. The sand stinging his face. The shrapnel hitting his back. *Oh, my God. John. Mick.*

A sudden jolt of pain sizzled through his left leg and onto a foot that wasn't there. Phantom pains, his doctors had called them. A royal pain in the ass threatening to ruin what was left of his life was the description Noah preferred.

As the current subsided, he snapped his eyes open, sucked in a shaky breath, and quickly glanced around. Instinctively, he reached under his jacket and touched the Beretta handgun he'd taken to carrying a few months after this last stint of being embedded with the U.S. military. Despite a cool spring breeze, sweat beaded on his upper lip. People walked by, laughing and chatting, oblivious to anything except the waffle cones in their hands.

You're safe now. Safe. There were no bombs on Mirabelle, he reminded himself. No insurgents. No terrorists. Here he could walk across the street without watching his back. He had a chance at holding down a full meal and sleeping at night. With any luck, the doctors would be right and the familiarity and comfort of his childhood home would help him climb out of this uncharacteristic hole.

He took another deep breath and released the gun. Several people walking toward him on the sidewalk nodded their greeting. Thankfully, they weren't locals. Best to get out of sight as quickly as possible.

Noah levered himself back up and continued slowly down the block. Although groups of people dotted the sidewalks and street, he remembered days when he hadn't been able to ride his bike due to the crowds. As he passed by the gift shop, he noticed paint chipping on the windowframe, and the carriage parked outside the medical clinic had seen better days. Apparently rough times had befallen a few residents.

An older woman, in her early sixties Noah guessed, walked briskly toward him. Immediately, he recognized her as Sally McGregor, the island's postmaster and one of the biggest grouches known to mankind. Rumor had it, at least while Noah had lived on Mirabelle, that she'd been known to trap and kill rabbits eating her gardens, kick dogs making messes on the sidewalk in front of her post office, and hand out poisoned apples to any kids ballsy enough to knock on her door at Halloween.

Her gaze settled on his leg for a moment and then flitted uncomfortably away. She didn't recognize him, but she knew. He was a cripple. He wasn't whole like her. *Yeah, well, we've all got challenges, don't we?*

On the cobblestone street, a bike rider headed toward him, her metal basket filled with cut flowers of every imaginable color. The sight was a little too charming, if you asked him.

As she came closer, she smiled and nodded.

"Morning." Noah tipped his head. He could be as cordial as the next guy, when he forced himself.

She braked to a stop at the curb. "Well, I'll be a son of a gun!" It was Mrs. Miller, owner of the ice cream shop, and, since he'd worked for her one summer, one of the few people on the island who'd been nice to him. "Noah Bennett? Is that you?"

"Yes, ma'am." Apparently all that time embedded with U.S. soldiers had rubbed off on Noah in more ways than one. He rested a hand on the black corner lamppost and stood a little straighter. Hopefully, she wouldn't notice his bad leg. "Hello, Mrs. Miller."

"Oh, my. How long's it been since you've been home?"

"Close to fifteen years."

"You haven't changed a bit."

Right.

"Still the spitting image of your mother." She shook her head. "Does your dad know you're here?"

Noah felt his smile wane. "No, ma'am."

She didn't know how to respond to that, and he couldn't blame her. The truth was that other than right after the explosion when Noah had been in the hospital, he couldn't remember the last time he'd spoken with his father.

Worry lines creased Mrs. Miller's already wrinkled brow. "How long will you be in town?"

He shrugged. "Not sure."

"Are you feeling all right? You look a little pale." That's when she seemed to make a connection. Her gaze shot to his tennis shoes and back up again.

Had his dad told everyone? Even Isaac and Sophie? *Dammit.* The last thing he wanted was pity. "I'm fine."

"Well, if there's anything I can do for you, let me know." She put her feet back on the pedals and sped away.

Wonderful. The first thing Mrs. Miller was going to do when she got back to her store was call all her cronies. So much for a couple days of anonymity.

He'd taken no more than two steps when a young couple came barreling out of the flower shop and bumped into him. He recognized the woman's bright pink jacket from the ferry. If memory served, these two had been the last to board over at the mainland and amongst the first off upon arrival at Mirabelle.

The guy turned around. "Sorry."

"No problem." Noah glanced into his face. *Holy crap.* Marty Rousseau. All grown-up. Of all the people—

"Noah?" Marty said. "Is it really you? Geez, I can't believe it!"

Mrs. Miller was one thing, but Noah was not ready for this. He gave a moment's thought to turning around and walking away without a word, but Marty didn't deserve that. "Hey, Marty." He held out his hand.

Marty ignored it and, laughing, pulled Noah into a tight hug with his free arm. "How the hell have you been?" He slapped him a couple times on the back and stepped away.

"All right."

"I can't believe you're actually here!" He presented the pretty young blonde by his side. "This is my fiancée, Brittany."

"Glad to meet you." She smiled and energetically shook his hand. "How do you two know each other?" she asked. "Did you grow up on Mirabelle, too? Does he know Soph—"

Marty stopped her with a hand to her shoulder. "Noah is…was…the closest thing I've ever had to a brother." And that was about as much as either could offer at the moment by way of an explanation. "We're getting married in a couple weeks."

"Congratulations."

"I'll send you an invite so you have all the specifics." Marty's smile returned. "You have to come."

No effing way. "Maybe." They stood awkwardly for a few moments, Noah hoping for as normal a stance as possible.

"Marty?" the carriage driver yelled. "You got your flowers? Ready to head out?"

Noah glanced back. Arlo Duffy. His beard was grayer than Noah remembered, but who could forget that lean, iconic face. The man had had more pictures taken and published of him manning his carriages than any other islander doing anything.

"Be right there, Arlo!" Marty yelled back. "Brittany, why don't you get us a seat on the carriage? I'll be right there." He turned back to Noah. "How long will you be on the island?"

"I'm not sure. A few weeks, maybe more."

"You staying at the inn?" he asked.

Good God, no. "Grandma's place." Why he'd kept the cottage after she'd willed it to him was anyone's guess.

"Marty, honey?" his fiancée called from the carriage. "Let's go."

"Coming." Marty squeezed Noah's shoulder. "Listen. We'll be having wedding festivities all week at the inn for our guests—horseback riding, lawn games, sailing. Come on down sometime, okay? I'd love to catch up." He grinned as he jumped onto the carriage. "And beat you at a game of table tennis."

Noah nodded and forced a smile, although he had absolutely no intention of getting anywhere near the inn. "Good seeing you again, Marty." That, at least, was the truth.

The carriage pulled away from the curb and headed down Island Drive toward the Mirabelle Island Inn. Toward Sophie. It might take Marty a while to work up to it, but he'd eventually tell his sister that Noah was back on the island. Then what?

Noah had dealt okay with running into Marty. He could even fathom the possibility of seeing his dad after all these years, but Sophie? And Isaac? He looked down at his lifeless foot.

He thought he'd prepared himself. Over the past several weeks, since the doctors had convinced him that this was what he needed, he'd gone over it and over it. What he'd say, how he'd say it. What he'd do, wouldn't do. Now he got it. Preparing for his return to Mirabelle? There was no such thing.

CHAPTER TWO

SOPHIE ROUSSEAU SAT AT her desk, a Louis XV dining table an ancestor had brought over from France, and contemplated the dismal occupancy reports for the Mirabelle Island Inn on her computer screen. Less than two weeks from the start of tourist season and she wasn't even close to full capacity. It'd been a nail-biting spring as the reservations had trickled in more slowly than normal, and if things didn't pick up soon she'd have a hard time breaking even for the season.

"Sophie?" Jan Setterberg, the inn's general manager, breezed into the sun-filled room and dropped off the day's mail. "The three o'clock ferry passed by a few minutes ago."

Sophie glanced at her watch. "Is it that time already?" So engrossed in work, she'd forgotten her baby brother, Marty, and his fiancée, Brittany, were coming today to help prepare for the arrival next week of their wedding guests.

"You've got a couple minutes before the carriage makes its way here." Jan picked up Marty and Brittany's wedding invitation from the corner of Sophie's desk and studied the hand-painted watercolor design of wood violets and white lilacs. "Brittany's parents must have paid a small fortune for these."

"Nope." Sophie quickly shut down her computer. "Marty's not letting them pay for anything." After struggling financially for years, her brother's Internet brainchild had recently been bought out for a tidy sum. If he and Brittany had wanted, they could have treated the entire wedding party along with all their guests to a trip to Hawaii or Europe. "I hope Brittany's happy with Mirabelle."

"Rousseau weddings have been held on this island," Jan stated the historic detail with the cadence of a commercial sound bite, "since Jean Paul Rousseau took Marie Le Blanc to be his bride—"

"Back in 1715." As if Sophie needed the reminder. "I know. I know."

All her life, Sophie had breathed and dreamed Rousseau family tradition. From the time she was little, she'd sit on her father's lap and beg him to recount how Jean Paul and Marie had built the first inn on Mirabelle, how the voyageurs had sometimes passed through trading furs and stories, or how her ancestors had been friends with the Chippewa.

Even now, long after her parents had passed away, she'd held fast to their ideals, from the cassoulets, goose foie gras and Bordeaux on the restaurant menus to day-to-day operations. The Mirabelle Island Inn was as modern as could be when it came to computers, Web sites, phone and reservation systems, but not a hand soap, bedspread or plate was purchased without consideration of her fur-trading forebears who had settled the island back in the late 1600s.

The only tradition-breaking allowed at the inn was for weddings. On those occasions, the wishes of the bride and groom ruled. Normally, Sophie would be managing any wedding activities at the inn, but since this was Marty's event and she'd have family in town her staff would be taking charge.

"Don't you worry about a thing," Jan said. "Everyone's pulling out the stops for Marty and Brittany. That new wedding planner, Sarah, is a gem. Josie planned a spectacular menu for the entire week. I'll keep the guests busy with all kinds of fun activities. And they'll all be gone before the summer tourist season gets in full swing. You won't have to do much of anything except relax and enjoy yourself for a change."

"Okay, *Mom*." She might pay the salaries around this place, but her employees, the entire island for that matter, were more extended family than anything. "A few days off before the summer rush sounds good to me."

"Oh, before I forget." Jan held out samples of wallpaper designs. "I need your decision on new paper for the front desk area."

Sophie didn't need to mull over that one. "Replace it with the same print."

"I've said it before. I'll say it again." Jan waved the samples in front of Sophie. "We could use some contrasting color out there."

Most people assumed she didn't like change. Sophie preferred to think of herself as a stickler for historic details. "There's plenty of color. It's called green. Nice try though."

"Mom?" Two young voices sounded in unison from the direction of the lobby.

"In here, guys!"

Flip-flops and tennis shoes echoed loudly in the otherwise quiet hall as her daughter and son made their way toward her office. Lauren breezed into the room first, her long, dark blond hair flying behind her, dropped her backpack on the floor and plopped into one of two ornately carved, gilded chairs. Kurt walked in next and fell into the other chair, his curly light brown hair ruffled from the wind.

"Last day of school!" Lauren exclaimed and met Kurt's closed fist in the air with one of her own. "Yes!"

"I thought there was an end-of-the-year party," Sophie said. "Aren't you guys going?"

"Are you serious?" Lauren's face scrunched up with distaste. "All they're gonna do is play kissing games. Eww."

"Oh, yeah!" Kurt smiled and nodded. "I'm going."

"You'll kiss anyone." Lauren rolled her eyes.

"I wouldn't kiss you."

Despite being twins, Lauren and Kurt's personalities were as different as cold from hot, making for great entertainment. Sophie could sit back and watch them interact all day long.

"Oh, come on, Lauren," Jan said. "There must be someone at school you like."

"There are eight kids in my ninth-grade class, and I've known them my entire life." Lauren gave Jan a look she'd perfected in her fourteen short years, a cross between supreme condescension and youthful arrogance. "I still remember Ben peeing in his pants in kindergarten. Nate threw up last year during social studies. And Zach?" She folded her arms across her developing chest. "Still picks his nose."

Sophie kept from smiling by biting the inside of her cheek. Having grown up on the ten-square-mile island, she remembered feeling the exact same way about every boy. Except Noah.

"Those are my options," Lauren continued, turning from Jan to glare at Sophie. "If you don't get me off this island, Mom, I'm gonna die never having been kissed!"

"Lauren—"

"I'm serious!"

"Drama queen," Kurt charged.

"Indiscriminate kisser," Lauren shot back.

"Hey, hey, hey! We don't have time to argue. Marty and Brittany just got in on the last ferry."

Lauren jumped up from the chair. "Brittany's here? Now?"

"I thought the wedding stuff doesn't start for another week," Kurt said.

"They wanted some time to settle in and help get ready for their guests."

"Awesome!" Kurt said.

Sophie stood. "Should we meet them out front?"

"Definitely." The twins headed for the door.

Sophie followed, then stopped, looking back at Jan. "In case I forget, thanks for everything you're doing for Marty."

Jan smiled. "You're welcome."

Sophie caught up with Lauren and Kurt in the empty lobby. With dark green carpeting and pale green-and-rose printed wallpaper, one had the impression of walking into a garden. An awfully green garden. Maybe Jan was right. For a moment she considered some red accents to perk up the place.

But it's always been green.

She swung one arm around each of the kids' shoulders and headed outside. "Pretty exciting, huh? There hasn't been a Rousseau wedding on the island for years."

"There's *no way* I'm living here," Lauren said, "but I *am* getting married here."

"You have to kiss someone first." Kurt ran ahead.

"Oh, shut up." Lauren shot after him.

The moment Sophie stepped away from the entryway awning the late May sunshine hit her full in the face. She put a hand out to shield her eyes and perused the grounds, making sure all was in order for the fast approaching tourist season.

Irises bloomed along the front porch, ivy made its springtime creep up the east wall, and the lawns and hedges were trimmed to perfection. Pink and red geraniums and dahlias of every imaginable hue lined the walkways, and a row of purple lilacs in full bloom set a colorful backdrop to a flowing fountain. Even the rose garden, with its shrubs, topiaries and delightful climbing varieties, was budding out.

The gardener was doing an excellent job keeping the landscape alive and well and looking exactly as Sophie's great-grandmother had planned some one hundred years ago. Add to the mix a few details from her parents' wills, and the grounds would remain virtually unchanged for at least another century.

After they'd died, the inn property and over four hundred adjacent acres of undeveloped land had been put in trust for the Rousseau children: Sophie, Marty and their two sisters, Elizabeth and Jacqueline, who were both married and too busy raising families in suburban Minneapolis to care much one way or another about what was happening on Mirabelle.

Sophie earned a more than fair salary for running the inn, but she couldn't materially alter the premises, nor could the adjoining land be developed without unanimous approval from all four siblings. That was fine by Sophie.

She glanced beyond the manicured perfection and rested her eyes on the bordering wildness of craggy oaks and pines, some older than the inn itself. No wonder their little island had become a wedding destination for the Upper Midwest. No place mixed quaint with quiet better than Mirabelle.

She drew in a deep, satisfied breath and caught up with the kids farther down the drive. Past the row of blue spruce lining the road, the clip-clop of hooves on the cobblestone road sounded Marty and Brittany's arrival. The only motorized vehicles on the island were the ambulance and fire trucks, requiring guests and their luggage to be transported by horse-drawn carriages.

Lauren waved the minute Marty and Brittany appeared. Kurt, on the other hand, was far too cool to show his excitement. The carriage turned into the drive, and the moment the horses stopped, Brittany jumped up and—there was no other word for it—squealed. "I'm so excited! This island is perfect for a wedding. Thank you so much for agreeing to have this here. It's the best wedding present *ever.*"

Sophie grinned. Brittany had taken a little getting used to, and Sophie had worried that a twenty-two-year-old was too young for Marty, but after seeing how Brittany's zest complemented Marty's sober personality, liking her had been easy.

"Take a breath, sweetheart." Marty hopped out of the carriage and reached for Brittany's hand, helping her down.

Brittany's feet no sooner touched the ground than she turned and hugged Sophie. "You're going to be the best sister-in-law any new bride could ask for." Then it was Kurt's turn. "Kurt!" She drew the reluctant teenager into a brief hug. "I can't wait to see you in a tux. You'll look so handsome." She turned to Lauren and squealed again. "Lauren!" The two clasped their arms around each other. "I'm so excited. Aren't you excited?"

"I can't wait to see your dress!"

"I'll show it to you as soon as I unpack."

"Oh, your nails look gorgeous," Lauren murmured.

"Do you want me to do yours? I can do yours."

"Would you?"

Kurt looked at Marty and rolled his eyes.

Marty laughed as he grabbed their luggage from the back of the carriage. "Thanks, Arlo."

"See you later, Arlo," Sophie yelled.

"Ayep." He took off the carriage brake and tapped his reins.

Marty turned to Kurt. "Hey, slugger, how you doing?" They went through the motions of some funky handshake they'd made up the last time Marty had visited. When he turned to Sophie for a hug his gaze turned serious. "Hey, Sophie." There had to be something more than the normal prewedding jitters on his mind.

"What's the matter?" she whispered.

"Later," he whispered back.

After all the hellos, Brittany started up again, like a wind-up toy. "Everything is so beautiful. These gardens and grounds! They're looking better than ever. The photographer's going to love this. I love this! Oh, Marty!" She looked up at him and her eyes sparkled. "We're going to have such a perfect week."

He kissed her forehead. "Why don't you and Lauren go find Jan? She'll know our room numbers."

"That's a great idea." Brittany grabbed Lauren's arm.

"Then we can unpack your dress!" Lauren exclaimed, her head tilting toward Brittany's as they walked to the inn.

Kurt shook his head at Marty. "Does she ever stop chattering?"

"Are you kidding? That sweet music lulls me to sleep and nudges me awake every day, and I wouldn't have it any other way." Marty laughed at the sudden grimace on Kurt's face. "Just wait. That bug'll bite you someday."

"Not for a while yet," Sophie cautioned.

"Can I go to the party now?" Kurt asked.

"Grab a bag first, eh?" They carried Marty and Brittany's luggage to the main lobby entrance.

After Kurt took off on his bike Sophie turned to Marty. "Okay, out with it. What's going on?"

Clearly uncomfortable, he ran his hands through his hair and shifted from foot to foot. "You're not going to like this."

"I've had so many wedding upsets through the years, nothing fazes me anymore."

"It's not that." He shook his head, hesitating. "There was someone on the ferry just now. Someone I didn't expect to see." He looked straight into her eyes and then away as if he couldn't stand to see her reaction.

"Who?"

"Noah Bennett."

Noah? Sophie's mouth turned dust dry. Though she hadn't heard his name spoken aloud for years the sound of it still hurt. "This ferry? Today?"

Marty nodded.

"You sure it was him?"

"Positive."

"Did you talk to him?"

"Briefly."

"Why'd he come back?"

"He didn't say."

"Where's he staying?"

"Grandma Bennett's."

Just up the hill from the inn. Too close for her comfort, but it made sense given the old woman had willed the property to Noah when she'd died, hoping to lure him home, at least every once in a while. She shouldn't have bothered. He hadn't even come back for her funeral.

"Why is he here?" she asked. "Why now?"

Marty shrugged. "He looks like he's in pretty rough shape, like he could use some company. I…I hope it's all right. I…asked him to come down some time this coming week. To join in with the wedding activities…"

Although Marty kept talking his voice barely penetrated her thoughts. Fifteen years she'd waited to give Noah Bennett a piece of her mind, and now the moment was at hand.

"Sophie?" Marty touched her arm. "You okay?"

"Not even close." She spun away from her brother and marched toward Bennett Hill.

"Well, don't do anything stupid," Marty yelled. "Sophie!"

"When I get back, Marty," she shouted over her shoulder, "you can define *stupid* for me!"

PINK RHODODENDRONS AND buttercup lilies flowered along the front of the house, and purple irises sprouted along the south side. Gingerbread trim, wide porch, old-fashioned swing, big shade trees. The sight of Grandma Bennett's house poured a thick layer of calm over Noah's ragged nerves.

As he walked up the front steps, he noticed bushes in dire need of pruning and chipped and peeling siding and trim. The place had surely seen more pampered days. He retrieved the key from under a large planter where his grandmother had always left it and, propping open the storm door with his good leg, unlocked the solid oak front door.

Apparently, his dad hadn't gotten rid of anything since Grandma died. Everything looked pretty much the same, from the antique cherry furniture in the dining room and floral sofa in the living room to the white ruffled curtains and the red-and-white, circa-1950 table and vinyl chairs in the kitchen. Any minute now Noah half expected to see his grandma coming toward him, wiping her hands on her flower-printed apron.

Although he'd felt horrible for missing her funeral, there'd been no easy way out of the guerilla camps in the jungles of South America. She would have understood, better than anyone.

Noah left the heavy oak door open so air could flow through the screen on the top half of the storm door. He walked into the living room, sat on the couch and breathed a sigh of relief. After tugging up his pant leg, he rolled down the silicone sleeve holding the prosthetic to his leg and let the damned heavy thing drop to the floor.

He'd no sooner set his handgun within reach on the coffee table and sat back when his cell phone rang. Sliding it out of his back pocket, he answered, "Bennett here."

"It's Liz." As in Elizabeth Ingram, his editor and the closest thing he had to a friend these days. "Where are you?"

"Mirabelle."

"Good." She was quiet for a moment. Most people weren't aware the woman could just as easily tear a man apart as spoon-feed him chicken noodle soup at his hospital bedside. She sure had shocked the hell out of Noah. Having married her husband late in life, she'd never had children. Noah supposed he was the closest thing she'd ever have to a son. "Have you eaten anything today?" she asked.

"Yes." Lies were easiest. "So what's up?"

"We can extend your deadline another two months."

"I told you I need at least four."

"That would mean moving the release date. I won't do that. Too many wheels are already in motion."

"I can't do it, Liz." He might have three-quarters of the book already written, but since the explosion he hadn't touched the manuscript. It wasn't likely the rest of it was going to write itself.

"Do me a favor," she said. "Take several days on this island, maybe a few weeks, to clear your head. Then give it a shot, okay?"

He supposed he owed her at least that. "I'll try."

After ending the call, he closed his eyes and let his head fall back against the couch. His thoughts drifted. He had no idea how long he'd been out when a noise penetrated his senses. He shot forward and reached for the gun before his grandmother's possessions reoriented him and he relaxed. *Don't need it, dude.* It was only someone coming up the sidewalk.

Not wanting anyone to see him without his prosthetic, he quickly hopped on his one good leg across the room. When he saw her through the screen, he stopped. "Sophie." He should've known she'd come.

She faltered halfway up the steps. "Hello, Noah."

God, what a sight. He wished he had his camera. High on the hill as they were, the treetops, with their spring leaves, framed her face, a face that had barely changed after all these years. Her eyes held a few laugh lines, but their color was as green as he remembered. Even her hair was still as dark as midnight.

He grabbed the doorframe for balance and hoped like hell she stayed outside. "How have you been?"

"What are you doing here?" she asked.

That was cold, abrupt. "I'm guessing Mirabelle's lost its Welcome Capital of the World status."

"Why now? What do you want, Noah?"

She never had been one to fake nice. That's one of the reasons he'd liked her so much. Amidst the trappings of this fairyland, she'd been so real. "I don't want anything, Sophie. From anybody. Just leave me alone."

"Why can't you be alone on someone else's island?"

"Why are you so pissed off?"

She narrowed her eyes. "One day you ask me to marry you and the next day you're gone?"

"You turned me down, Sophie."

"And you never said goodbye."

"Ooh," he groaned, shaking his head. "I said goodbye all right. For three days and nights in that Bayfield motel room." Tenderly, passionately, fast, slow, laughing and crying. It was the only time in his entire life four walls hadn't closed in on him. "At least, that's the way I remember it."

She looked down, as if trying desperately to wipe the images from her mind. "I needed to hear the words."

"You knew I was leaving, Sophie. With…or without you." If he'd really loved her and if she'd really loved him, they'd have found a way to be together. True love always found a way. Well, Sophie had found her way all right. Without Noah.

"No phone calls. No letters." The fire was back in her eyes. "Nothing for damned close to fifteen years."

"Well, it sure as hell didn't take you long to replace me." It couldn't have been much more than a few months after Noah had left that she'd married his brother, Isaac. His own brother. Self-righteous anger boiled to the surface. "Married, two kids. Sounds like you and Isaac got along fine without me."

Her face flaming, she stalked across the porch.

"Don't!" He reached for the knob, but she was quicker.

She yanked open the screen door, cranked her hand back to slap him and stopped. Her gaze flew downward. She took in the one empty leg of his jeans and her fingers collapsed into a fist.

"Go ahead," he said, through clenched teeth. "Hit me! I'm sure I deserve it."

"You're an asshole, you know that?"

Yeah, he knew.

"Isaac died more than two years ago." She let the storm door slam shut and pounded off the porch.

CHAPTER THREE

ISAAC. DEAD?

After climbing the hill toward the small cemetery behind Mirabelle's only church, Noah reached the wrought-iron gate, his hands shaking, his breathing uneven, his thoughts disjointed. He couldn't believe his older brother was gone.

Looking past the weathered tombstones of the island's first settlers, the names engraved there as familiar to him as his own, he located the Bennett family headstone, a pale gray granite monstrosity, and forced himself to close the distance, one slow step at a time.

Though the cemetery was well-maintained, short grass infringed on the edges of the ground markers and dirt partially obscured the names. The middle two granite slabs were his grandparents. The two on the left were an aunt who'd died as a child and an uncle who'd been killed in military service. The marker on the right was new.

Noah fell awkwardly to his knees and brushed the granite clean. *Isaac Andrew Bennett.* Seeing his brother's name, his birthday and date of death didn't make the truth any more real. This had to be a bad dream. It had to be. Shit like this had happened to him over and over again in that damned hospital. Any minute he'd awaken from this nightmarish sleep. Any minute. He squeezed his eyes closed, hoping that when he opened them he'd be anywhere but on Mirabelle. *Wake up. Wake up.*

A robin chirped cheerfully from the branches of a nearby maple, and the sounds of a lawn mower buzzed in the distance. The scent of lilacs hung in the still, warm air. This was real. Very real. His older brother was dead. Gone.

Snippets of memories flashed through Noah's mind. Isaac and him fighting over what to watch on TV, fishing off the pier and snowshoeing. Isaac had always wanted to go traipsing through the snow in the midst of the most miserable blizzards. He'd loved being outside, especially in winter, and he'd loved this island, almost as much as Noah hated it.

How could two brothers be so different? Even in the trouble-making department they were like night and day. Oh, they'd both caused plenty of it. Creeping through this cemetery on Halloween and scaring the younger kids. Raiding McGregor's apple trees. Toilet-papering the Andersens' place. He could go on and on recalling the shenanigans he and Isaac had pulled. But no matter what they'd done together, Noah had always been the one who'd gotten caught. Trouble had a way of sliding off Isaac like water on a duck's back. Except for this time.

Noah traced the engraved letters of Isaac's name on the granite slab and, inside him, sadness over the loss warred with anger over what Isaac had done. He'd never forgiven his brother for marrying Sophie, and now he wasn't sure he'd ever forgive him for dying before Noah had gotten the chance to speak his mind, before he'd been able to find it inside himself, if that was possible, to forgive his brother and move on.

"Isaac," he said aloud. "What the hell?"

A horse snuffled somewhere behind him and Noah started at the sound. Adrenaline rushed through him as if nothing less than a gun was pointed at his head.

You're on Mirabelle, he reminded himself. *You're safe. Safe.* He took a deep breath and turned around.

This, Noah did not need. Mirabelle Island's Chief of Police, Jim Bennett, reined in his horse and stopped at the entrance to the cemetery. Apparently the island rumor mill had been working at lightning speed.

The chief dismounted and walked across the grounds, only to tower over where Noah knelt in the grass. Fifteen plus years of distance made the man no less intimidating. "Hello, Noah."

"Dad." Noah glanced at Isaac's marker and barely held the tears in check. "How'd it happen?"

"He was shot during a raid on an illegal fishing operation."

Isaac, always the devoted son, had followed family tradition of military service or law enforcement and become a game warden. In idyllic northern Wisconsin, arresting deer poachers should've been the most dangerous part of his job. Instead, he'd been murdered over fish. Fish. It didn't make any sense. None of it made any sense.

"Did Sophie… Did he make it to a hospital?"

"No. He was hit in the chest. Died instantly at the scene."

Noah looked away. The thought of his brother shot and killed violently like so many soldiers he'd seen through the years was too much. "Why didn't you tell me?"

"Couldn't find you. I called your editor, your agent. Every number I had. After a while, it didn't seem to matter."

Noah glanced at the date on the marker. He'd been in the mountains of either Afghanistan or Pakistan, about as unreachable as he'd ever been. Still, an urgent message could've made it to Noah through the military. After all these years, his dad knew that. He hadn't wanted Noah to come back, that much was obvious.

"I should have been here," Noah said. "I would've wanted to be here. That wasn't right."

"I figured if you'd wanted to stay in touch," his dad said, "you'd have checked in."

The first years after he'd left Mirabelle, Noah had called every so often. Other than news of happenings on Mirabelle his dad rarely had anything to say. Eventually, Noah didn't have anything to say, either, and there was a lot of dead air. He'd resorted to occasional letters, even though they often hadn't been acknowledged.

"So what're you doing here now?" his dad asked.

Noah debated, lies or the truth? For some reason a lie seemed appropriate. With a cop for a father, he'd gotten good at it at a very early age. "Thought I'd check up on Grandma's place. See if there was anything that needed doing."

His dad mulled that one over and didn't seem to be buying it.

"And I needed to stay relatively close to the Mayo Clinic in Rochester," Noah added for good measure. "It's a little easier to get there from here than Rhode Island." They wanted him to check in with a physical therapist, but he'd be damned if he'd go. He'd had enough of doctors, nurses and the like to last several lifetimes.

"How long you planning on staying?" The tone of his dad's voice made the innocent enough question sound more like, "When're you leaving?"

Why Noah had expected anything different was beyond him. "No more than a month or two. Why?" Sick of looking up at his father, he eased himself up onto his good foot. He was inordinately pleased to notice that he'd actually grown quite a bit taller than his dad. Jim Bennett had, of course, aged. He'd put on some pounds around the waist, deep wrinkles marked his forehead and his hair had thinned and turned completely gray. Only his mustache held any remnants of his original dark hair. "You ready to escort me to the ferry dock, tell me to get the hell off your island and never come back?"

"No." His dad ignored the bait, glancing instead at Noah's legs, his jaw clenching with some unknown emotion.

"What is it then?" Noah asked, raising his voice. Fifteen years had gone by and he still felt himself falling right back into the old argumentative patterns. No one could cut Noah deeper or quicker than Jim Bennett. "What did I ever do to hurt you?" Noah asked. "It can't be because I didn't go into law enforcement, or do a military stint. You hated me long before that."

His dad's gaze flew to Noah's face. "I don't hate you."

"Then what is it, Dad? I want to know."

As if Noah hadn't said a word his dad mounted his horse. "Stay as long as you like, Noah. As long as you like."

JIM BENNETT PACED HIS KITCHEN floor waiting for night to fall. All he could think about was the sight of Noah kneeling at Isaac's grave. His eyes watered, blurring the image. *Dammit.* There were two things parents should never have to do, outlive their own children and be forced to make a choice between themselves and their own flesh and blood.

Feeling as if he might wear a track in the linoleum, he stopped in front of the sink and glanced out the window. "Oh, hell," he murmured to himself. "It's dark enough."

Taking off out the back door of his house, he quickly headed four blocks down the street and then cut through the woods. The moment he caught sight of the gray-and-white cottage with its wide front porch and four-season addition off the side, his shoulders relaxed and the knot in his stomach loosened. He knocked on the front door.

A moment later, Josie appeared, her knitting bag in hand. "How many times do I have to tell you, Jim, that you don't need to knock."

"It's your house."

"Which is why I gave you a key."

He made to step inside.

"I was just on my way out to sit on the porch." She flicked on the porch light, stepped outside and headed toward the swing.

"No. Let's go inside."

"You go inside." Josie sat down and pulled out her latest project, a pair of socks for her granddaughter living in eastern Iowa. "After spending the entire day in that kitchen getting ready for Marty's wedding I need the fresh air." Being head cook at the Mirabelle Island Inn, she'd be taking the brunt of an influx of close to a hundred people for Marty's wedding. "It's a beautiful night, and I'm going to guess you could use the fresh air."

Jim glanced uneasily around. "All right. Fine. Have it your way." He flicked off the porch light, cutting down the chances of anyone seeing him here at Josie's this late at night. The jaws on this island were flapping about his business enough as it was with Noah coming home.

"How do you expect me to see what I'm knitting?"

"You can make a pair of socks in your sleep." As if to prove his point, her needles clicked away, never missing a beat.

What he hated most about the island gossip chain was when the rest of the island knew about things that concerned him before he did. They'd known when Isaac had been given a scholarship to college. When Noah had broken his arm falling out of one of the Rousseaus' trees. They'd all guessed Sophie was pregnant before the thought had occurred to Jim. They'd even known about Gloria leaving.

He'd been at his desk when Herman's wife had called. Arlo had said something to his wife, Lynn, about Gloria going on a vacation. He'd taken her to the pier with several suitcases. Lynn had called someone, that someone had called several other someones, and in no time the entire island had been privy to one of Jim's greatest failures. Who could blame him for wanting to keep parts of his life private?

He sat on the swing next to Josie, took his pipe and pouch out of his front pocket and packed some tobacco. A moment later, he struck a match, puffed and let go a long sigh.

"Have you seen him yet?" Josie asked.

There was no need to specify Noah. He knew. "Found him out at the cemetery late this afternoon."

Her hands paused.

He took another puff on his pipe and stared out at the half moon rising over Lake Superior. "Isaac dying was bad. The worst thing I've ever gone through. But I'm telling you, Josie, seeing Noah kneeling at his brother's grave…about brought me to my knees," he said, his voice cracking.

She put her hand on his leg.

There was no doubt that Noah coming home after all this time was nothing short of bittersweet for Jim. His conscience gnawed at the lining of his stomach. "Maybe I should've tried harder to find him. A man deserves to bury his own brother."

Then again, Noah coming home would've opened up a whole big can of worms. *Nope.* Noah had made his bed when he'd left. Jim might have to atone for other things, but not telling Noah about Isaac dying wasn't one of them. "I guess Noah being here for the funeral wouldn't have changed anything. He couldn't have brought Isaac back."

"Wasn't there any part of you happy to see your own son?"

"Happy? Sure. I suppose." He puffed on his pipe. "He's a man now, Josie. I've seen pictures of him in magazines and on the backs of his books, but that's nothing like seeing him in person. He's bigger than Isaac and built differently. His shoulders are broader. But seeing him limp on that fake leg? I sure as hell wasn't ready for that."

"How did he seem?"

"Oh, hell, he hasn't changed. Not one damned bit. Still as angry as ever. Still hates me."

"He doesn't hate you."

"Coulda fooled me. Since the day Gloria left he's been ornery and contrary. I say black, he says white. I don't think he'll ever change." Jim had always wondered if Noah hadn't blamed him for Gloria leaving, and he wouldn't have been too far off the mark.

"You still angry at him?"

"Angry? I don't know." He shook his head. "I'll tell you what, though, he's still the spitting image of Gloria. Those two were like peas in a pod."

"Well, there you have it." Her needles clicked on. "You divorced Gloria, didn't you?"

SOPHIE COULDN'T SLEEP. She lay in bed, telling herself that it probably had to do with that late-afternoon diet cola, or nerves over Marty's wedding plans, an unanswered e-mail or other work-related issues. Excuses, all of them. A violent storm of thoughts whirled through her head, making it impossible for her to shut down. How unlike her to not be able to disconnect. Shutting down was an art she'd perfected through the years. Why was it failing her now?

Noah. Her armor had been useless around him.

After flipping back the lightweight quilt, she dressed in sweats, checked on both kids to make sure they were sound asleep and set out into the warm night air for a walk. Other than Duffy's Pub and a couple other bars downtown, Mirabelle closed up after ten o'clock, so the only light illuminating her journey was a bright half moon and the dim, old-fashioned lampposts lining Island Drive. In truth, she probably could've made her way around this island in complete darkness, she knew it so well.

One mile led to another and, before Sophie knew it, she found herself taking an overgrown path toward the lighthouse. *The* lighthouse. Hers and Noah's. Old force of habit, she guessed, reinstating itself along with Noah's return.

No one usually went to the northeast side of the island. Surrounded as it was by undeveloped Wisconsin state parkland, this point was one of the few spots on the entire island a person could go and not worry about being bothered. None of the residents cared to hike this far off the main road and if visitors wanted lighthouse charm, the one in town was more easily accessible.

She cleared the white pine forest and looked out over the moonlit surface of the water. Ahead of her, like a postcard, the lighthouse stood sentinel on the island's rocky northeast peninsula. Although she hadn't been here in more than a decade, she and Noah had come here often, sneaking out of their houses late at night for time alone together. They'd stashed a blanket, lantern, sodas or a six-pack and food behind some bushes near the lighthouse foundation. How many hours had they lingered here talking about their future, where they'd go to college, where they'd live and, always, where they'd travel?

A lot of good it had done.

She picked her way over the barely discernible path toward a large, flat boulder at the water's edge, scooped up some rocks and skipped them across the relatively calm surface. Memories flooded in with every soft wave hitting the shore. The remembered sound of Noah's laughter echoed off the lighthouse and bounced off the water, free and unbound.

"I would've guessed you didn't come here anymore." The deep, masculine voice came from behind her.

She spun around and found Noah sitting with his back against the lighthouse, one leg stretched in front of him. "Sorry," he said. "Didn't mean to scare you."

The sight of him now was no less upsetting than when she'd first seen him at Grandma Bennett's house. She barely kept herself from charging over there and...and...kicking him. "Scare me? Hardly. And I haven't been here for years."

Why was she here now, anyway? It was bad enough Noah was back on the island, but coming here, to the place they'd first made love, what had she been thinking? She started across the rocks on her way back toward the road.

"I couldn't sleep, either," he said before she'd taken more than a step or two. "Too many memories." He was wearing a stocking cap and had a heavy wool blanket wrapped around him, making it look as if he planned on camping there for the night. It might have been the beginning of summer, but on big water like Lake Superior the nights could be cold even after the hottest of days.

Curiosity got the better of her. "How long have you been out here?"

"I don't know." He shrugged. "Couple hours."

Hours. Sitting at their lighthouse, remembering, reliving. When she looked into his tired eyes she understood. That didn't mean she was any less angry. She started again toward the road.

"Sophie?" he said. "I'm sorry."

She stopped. For what? She wanted to scream at him. For leaving me here all alone? For ruining my dreams and breaking my heart?

"About Isaac."

Oh. Isaac. Sadness dampened the rage.

"If I'd known," he said. "I'd have come back."

She heard him swallow and softened for a moment. As much

as she hated this man, he'd just discovered he'd lost his only sibling. "Your dad tried—"

"Not very hard, Soph. The military was always able, someway, somehow, to get urgent messages to me. He didn't want me coming back."

A small part of her had probably always wondered about that. "You being here wouldn't have changed anything."

"He was my brother. I should've been here to say goodbye. Regardless of the issues between all of us, I would've been here for you."

Then it was probably for the best that he hadn't been here for the funeral. There's no telling what kind of fool she'd have made of herself in that vulnerable state. But she wasn't vulnerable now. "Why now, Noah? Why the hell did you come back after all this time?"

He tossed a few rocks out into the water. "The truth?"

"What do you think?"

He studied her while he seemed to be deciding what, if anything, to say. "Okay," he said. "The truth. Since losing my foot, I can't sleep. When I do, I have constant nightmares. I can barely hold down a meal. I have a hard time concentrating. I can't write, can't take pictures. And I've got a book due in a couple months. I could lose my job, my career." He patted his prosthetic. "And I sometimes have what's called phantom pains that are almost worse than the pain after the actual explosion."

"In short, you're a basket case."

"It could be worse. I could develop a full-blown case of post-traumatic stress disorder. That's what my doctors are worried about. PTSD."

"So your doctors wanted you to come here?"

He nodded.

"Why? What's here for you? I don't get it."

He looked away. The only sound was that of the frigid waters of Lake Superior lapping against the rocks. "I don't know if you can understand," he said, sounding very tired.

"Try me."

He sighed. "Since leaving Mirabelle, I've pretty much moved from one war-torn region in the world to the next. I've been shot at more times than I can count and actually hit a couple times. I've been blindfolded and taken to secret rebel camps. Nearly kidnapped twice. Spent many nights wondering if I was going to be alive in the morning. After more than a decade in places like Bosnia, Sudan, Afghanistan and Iraq…" He paused. "Mirabelle is the only place…"

"You feel safe." For a moment, she tried putting herself in his shoes and, in spite of every intention to the contrary, sympathy pricked her conscience.

He wouldn't meet her eyes. "One full night's sleep, Sophie. I can't tell you what I'd do for a straight eight hours." The moonlight cast pale light over his face, making him look almost ghostly, but the dark circles under his eyes were painfully real.

That's when she noticed the unopened bottle of vodka next to him and wondered what he was waiting for. Maybe this end was no less than he deserved. "So am I supposed to feel sorry for you?"

"No." He shook his head. "You don't need to feel anything for me."

"How long are you staying?"

"As long as it takes."

That could be weeks. *Oh, my God, months.* She wasn't sure she could handle more than a few days. What about Lauren and Kurt? What if Noah started asking questions? The possibility made her stomach churn. She started again toward the road.

"Sophie—"

"I don't get it!" Unbidden, the words burst from her mouth.

"You never called! Never wrote," she said, needing to get this off her chest once and for all. "My dad died, and you left. You left!"

Her dad had suffered a massive heart attack and died right before she and Noah had graduated from high school. They'd been planning on heading off to college in the fall. Instead, she'd had to stay to help her mother with the inn. She'd had no choice. The Mirabelle Island Inn had been owned and operated by a Rousseau for hundreds of years, and her two sisters and Marty had been little more than teenagers at the time. Then her mother had gotten sick right after Noah had left and the decision had been all but taken out of her hands.

Overnight she'd gone from being on the cusp of seeing her dreams realized to having to run the inn and helping to take care of three younger siblings. And Noah? He'd left to make his dreams come true. Without her.

"You know I was the only one capable of helping my mom with the inn," she said. "We plan a lifetime together and one snag comes along and you're gone."

"Hell, Sophie," he said, sounding weary. "Back then every day on this island felt like an eternity to me. I had a college scholarship that was going to disappear if I didn't show up on campus that fall. I was eighteen. An impatient, stupid kid. If I could do it over again…" He paused. "I couldn't stay. You couldn't leave," he whispered. "No matter how much we want things to work out, Sophie, some things aren't meant to be."

"That's what you've told yourself all these years, isn't it, Noah. To clear your conscience."

"No, Sophie." He picked up a rock and angrily whipped it out into the water. "You marrying Isaac only a few months after I left took care of my conscience just fine."

Maybe she should've told him the truth back then. Maybe— No! Her spine stiffened. *He's the one who left. He made his choice when he walked off this island and never looked back.* "Well, at least I found out what you were made of before it was too late."

"What the hell is that supposed to mean?"

"That I obviously married the more dependable of the Bennett boys."

"Boy, you got that right," he bit back at her. "Now that we understand each other, I'll do my best to stay out of your way."

"You do that." As she stalked away the unmistakable sound of a cap opening on a bottle followed her. Maybe he'd drink that vodka, suffer hypothermia and die out here.

She should be so lucky.

CHAPTER FOUR

A WHITE-TAILED DEER BOLTED twenty feet in front of Sophie as she came close to finishing her usual five-mile morning run that twisted and turned through Mirabelle's undeveloped state land, continued with a jaunt straight through the Rousseau forest and ended back at the inn. A pair of gray squirrels scurried across the damp, leafy carpet and a woodpecker hammered after breakfast on a dying, if not already dead, pine tree that had been struck by lightning the previous summer.

She'd learned years ago to take the quiet morning hours for herself. Sometimes the kids or work took priority. More often than not, she reserved this precious time for walking or running through the forest, her wild sanctuary.

It was also the place that helped ground her in her ancestry. On windy days her father's quiet, but authoritative voice seemed to whisper through the treetops. *You're a part of this island, chérie… You more than anyone have to keep the Rousseau traditions alive.* And so she had, from the menu at the Fourth of July corn boil to the handmade Christmas decorations to the brand of New Year's champagne. She felt his approval every time she ran this path.

This morning, though, her run didn't have its usual calming effect. She couldn't seem to slow herself down and maintain a steady pace. Images of Noah, one legged, standing at

Grandma Bennett's door and sitting, wrapped in that blanket at the lighthouse, kept popping into her mind, driving her on, faster and faster.

She burst through the tree line and onto the inn grounds, slowed to a walk and glanced at her watch. Normally, she ran her five-mile track around the island in an hour, but this morning she'd finished in record time.

While stretching her arms and neck, she looked up the hillside and strained to see through the trees. Was Noah awake? Probably not. It was early. The sun was only now rising over Lake Superior. Curls of fog clung to the water's calm surface like a fuzzy blanket, and she couldn't help imagining him sleeping, couldn't help wondering if he still slept naked. That was a dangerous thought and a useless one at that.

She drew in a breath of the cool morning air before quietly entering her living quarters by the back door of the inn and peeking in on Kurt and Lauren. They were both snoozing away in their respective bedrooms, and what else should they be doing on their first day of summer break?

After showering and dressing, Sophie left a note on the kitchen table for the kids to check in at her office after they'd had breakfast, and then she entered the inn through the passageway into the kitchen.

Josie was busy at the stove, her thick black hair streaked with coarse gray strands drawn back in a large clip. Her white bib apron, fresh that morning and tied over a red T-shirt and khaki pants, had yet to become the least bit soiled.

"Morning, Josie."

"Good morning, Sophie. Your coffee's ready. Made an egg bake for Marty and his fiancée, or would you rather have your usual?"

She shrugged. "Whatever you've already cooked up will be

perfect. If you've got extras." She could live without oatmeal and fresh fruit for one morning.

Jim Bennett, Sophie's father-in-law, sat at the wide metal counter, sipping coffee. Every morning, provided there was time after his usual early morning fishing jaunt, he could be found in that exact location.

Jim and Josie were discreet about their relationship, but on an island this small nothing stayed secret for long. Jim had been divorced for decades, since Gloria had left, and Josie's husband had died several years ago. Why they didn't get married or move in together was anyone's guess.

Jim looked up from the Bayfield newspaper. "You're looking very relaxed today, Sophie."

And looks could be deceiving. She planted a kiss on his forehead and poured herself a cup of coffee. "I hate to say it, but you look tired."

"Nah, I'm fine."

His jacket smelled like sweet pipe tobacco and Sophie got a bit sentimental thinking about all this man had done for her through the years. She rubbed his shoulders. "Tense, too. I'm going to guess you've seen Noah."

Was it her imagination or had his shoulders tightened even more. "Yep," he murmured.

"You know, you could've warned me he was coming."

"I would have. If I'd known. The first I heard about it was from Lynn. Arlo told her after dropping Marty off and then she called the station."

Lynn was Arlo's wife. She ran Duffy's Pub and Arlo ran the stables and carriage business. Very little happened on this island without those two knowing about it.

Josie set a plate heaping with a baked mixture of scrambled eggs, sausage, cheese and veggies on the table in front of him and another plate with much smaller portions in front of Sophie. "You two eat before it gets cold."

"Thanks, Josie." She took a bite, but the food lodged in her throat. "Did you know about his accident?"

"That was no accident."

"But you knew?"

He nodded.

"Why didn't you tell me?"

Jim pursed his lips, considering. "I didn't want you feeling sorry for him."

That wasn't likely to happen any time soon. She glanced at Josie. "You knew, too, didn't you?"

She nodded.

"That means the whole island knows. Everyone except me. I can't believe neither one of you told me."

Jim ate a few forkfuls, but there was clearly something bothering him. He dropped his fork onto his plate. It clanged in the large open space of the industrial-sized kitchen. "Goddammit! I told him it would happen someday," Jim blurted out. "You can't flirt with disaster the way he has for years and not get burned."

"There's no point getting into this now," Josie said softly.

"Did you know, too, that his doctors are worried he might develop post-traumatic stress disorder?"

Jim shook his head. "When did you talk to him?"

"Last night. I went for a walk and ran into him."

"Don't you dare feel sorry for him, you hear me?" Jim pushed away his plate of food, stood and pulled on his jacket. "For your own good, stay away from Noah. He'll run again. Just like his mother."

"You think I don't know that?" she yelled. "You think I've forgotten how I felt when he left?"

The day she'd woken up alone in that Bayfield hotel room

she'd promised herself she would never again love any man the way she'd loved Noah Bennett. Completely, recklessly, passionately. "Never again, Jim. Never."

NOAH SAT ON THE FRONT PORCH swing holding a steaming cup of coffee in his hands, but after finishing off the better part of that bottle of vodka last night he wasn't sure he'd be able to hold anything down. Scraping and priming the house? Not in this lifetime. He could only stare at the paint peeling off the railing.

A screen door slammed from the vicinity of the inn and he wondered if Sophie was out and about. Seeing her at the lighthouse—their lighthouse—last night had about killed him. There were few places on this island not fraught with memories of their childhood, their friendship, their love, though the lighthouse—the place they'd first made love—was the most poignant of all. But he couldn't let himself remember what it'd felt like to hold her, make love to her. He'd been down that road before and all it had led to was physical and emotional agony.

Kids' voices coming up the hill sidetracked him, and he craned his neck to look over the porch rail. A boy and a girl. Sophie and Isaac's kids, no doubt.

A couple years after he'd left the island, his dad had told him they'd had children and that'd changed everything for Noah. Overnight, the desire to get as far away from Mirabelle, Sophie and Isaac as he could manage burned in his gut. He'd ended up taking an overseas journalism internship and from there traveled the world.

To hell with Sophie and Isaac, but the kids? Several times, he'd thought about sending Christmas presents or tokens of his travels to Kurt and Lauren, but in the end it had been too painful to make contact with his niece and nephew. He'd had to shut out the whole lot of them.

Sophie and Isaac. Married. Sharing their life together. Making love. Making babies. It hadn't made sense, then or now. Isaac had always wanted to have kids, but how could he have had sex with Sophie? How could she have had sex with his brother? It had all been too painful, and seeing the kids suddenly made it all too real.

"I'm going to Kally's. Where are you going?"

"Ben's. Then to Zach's."

"You have to be home for supper. It's your turn to do the dishes tonight."

"I washed 'em yesterday."

"No, you didn't!"

"Then what did we have for dinner? Huh? Huh?"

They looked like teenagers, but that couldn't be right. Mentally, he calculated back to when his dad had told him about the twins. They couldn't be older than eleven, maybe twelve.

What hit Noah first was how much Lauren's face reminded him of Sophie as a young girl. Darken the young girl's hair, put in some waves, and bam, young Sophie, ready to skip stones at the lighthouse, or kayak to one of the other Apostle Islands to explore the caves. Kurt, with his startling blue eyes, favored Isaac.

Dammit, Isaac. Why did you have to take Sophie? You had everything else.

Yeah, but you left her, you idiot.

Doesn't matter. She belonged to me.

You left. She stayed. She chose.

The twins walked across his grandmother's yard, apparently on the way to friends' houses, and came to a quick stop on seeing him sitting on the porch. Staring back at Noah, they seemed intensely curious, making him wonder what, if anything, Sophie had told them about him.

"Hey there," he said. "You must be Sophie's kids."

His niece and nephew. *Damn*. He was an uncle. Of sorts.

The girl nodded.

"You Noah?" the boy asked. His young voice, on the cusp of puberty, fluctuated from high to low and back again, as if unable to make up its mind. Grow up, or stay young?

Like a punch in his gut, Noah realized he'd been younger than Kurt when his mother had left. Noah had come home from school one afternoon to find his dad and Isaac sitting at the kitchen table. His dad had looked up at Noah and said, "Your mother left this morning, and, this time, she won't be coming back. What do you want for supper?" and that had been the extent of their conversation.

Sophie's mom had been the one to explain it to him. "It's not you, Noah, sweetheart," she'd said days later. "It's this island. A person either loves it, or she hates it."

It wasn't always as simple as that.

"Yep, I'm Noah." He nodded at the kids. "Lauren and Kurt?"

Lauren smiled and took a step or two toward the porch. "Marty said you're a writer."

So Marty, not Sophie, had been talking about him.

"No, he didn't," Kurt argued, keeping his distance on the lawn. "He said he's a photographer."

"Actually, I'm both."

"Will you be taking the pictures for Marty's wedding?" she asked.

"Not that kind of photographer."

"What other kind is there?"

"I'm a photojournalist. I travel, write books and articles, take pictures."

"I can't wait to travel," Lauren said. "I want to go every-where. Have you ever been to Tokyo?"

"Nope." There weren't any wars in Japan.

"Marty said you were in an explosion." Kurt was clearly intrigued. "A roadside bomb went off in Iraq."

Noah nodded.

"Ever been shot at?"

"A few times." Noah didn't bother telling Kurt about his stint covering civil unrest in Haiti. There was nothing heroic about sleeping in a bathtub while bullets zinged overhead. "I took two bullets in Afghanistan. Right here and here." He pointed once near his shoulder, again at his thigh. "Left a couple of nice scars." He'd been lucky. The bullets had missed bone and went clear through muscle. "I had a flak jacket on, otherwise I wouldn't be alive today."

More and more these days he was considering settling down at his house in Rhode Island and focusing on his books.

"Do you carry a gun?" Kurt's face lit up. "Did you ever see Osama bin Laden?"

"No, I've never seen bin Laden." He laughed, sidestepping the question about the gun. "But I was with our military forces when they were fighting the Taliban."

"Cool."

In some ways, yes. Others, definitely no.

The clip, clop, clip of a single horse's hooves drew their attention toward the rider coming up the hill. Dark blue uniform. Hat and shield. *Ah, hell. Now what?* Too early in the morning for this.

"Hi, Grandpa," the twins said, practically in unison, clearly comfortable in the man's presence.

"Hey, there, Miss Mirabelle," his dad said to Lauren. "Young man," he said, nodding to Kurt. "Morning, Noah." He took off his hat, and his mouth flattened.

"Morning, Dad."

His father turned back to the kids, love and tolerance abundant in his damned grandpa smile. Go figure. "Did you two remember to check in with your mom before heading out this morning?"

"No." Kurt rolled his eyes. Lauren put a somewhat defiant hand on her hip.

"Well, then you know exactly what you need to do before you head off to any friends' houses, don't you? Hop to it."

"We're having a bonfire tonight," Lauren said to Noah. "You should come."

Noah opened his mouth, but he wasn't sure how to politely decline.

"I'm sure Noah has other stuff going on, kids," the chief said.

"Maybe another night," Noah offered.

"Okay," Lauren said. "Marty said he wants one every night he's here."

"Later," Kurt said.

"Bye." Lauren's hair flew when she spun around and raced her brother down the hill.

"Nice kids."

The horse shook his big brown head, shifted, and his dad loosened the reins. "Isaac was a good dad. He and Sophie did okay." His dad cleared his throat and looked out over the great expanse of Lake Superior.

"Something on your mind, Dad?"

"Yeah. I think it's best if you steer clear of Sophie."

Noah wasn't exactly sure why, but this pissed him off more than anything else. He'd been a black sheep as far as these islanders were concerned, never fitting in, always wanting something different for his life, but he'd never been a serious troublemaker. He'd never thrown it in their faces.

"Sophie can decide for herself who she wants to be around," Noah said. "At least she always did in the past."

"Sophie's too softhearted for her own good, and you know it. With Isaac gone, I don't want you getting any ideas."

"You didn't want me to know he'd died, did you? You didn't want me coming back." Amazingly enough, his father's words and actions could still hurt.

"She doesn't need you messing up her life—"

"We were kids. Remember? I never messed—"

"Bullshit!" The horse snuffled and pawed a front hoof in the dirt as if reacting to its rider's anger. "Kids or not, she was hurt after you left. Until she and Isaac got together. No one on this island wants to see her go through that again. Not that you'd give a damn."

Noah barely held his temper in check. "I care about Sophie more than you could ever understand."

"You sure have a strange way of showing it."

"Why do you think I've stayed away all these years?"

"You and me never did get along. That doesn't have anything to do with Sophie."

"Not everything's about you, Dad."

The chief studied him, hard. "You're saying you stayed away from Mirabelle for Sophie's sake?"

Silently, Noah held his father's gaze.

"All right then." His dad set his hat back on his head and turned his horse toward the street. "At least we agree on one thing."

CHAPTER FIVE

"Got it!" Sophie yelled, positioning herself directly under the volleyball's trajectory. She popped the ball into the air, hoping to set it up for Marty, but she'd miscalculated.

"Dang, Sophie." Her brother had to dive to hit the ball over the net. "That was a close one."

"Sorry."

It was late Sunday afternoon and Marty was taking a break from all the wedding preparations for a friendly game of beach volleyball with Lauren, Kurt and Sophie. Sophie should have been relaxed, calm, having fun. She wasn't. The volleyball court faced inland toward Grandma Bennett's and she couldn't stop looking uphill.

"Game point," Marty said, grabbing the ball for his serve. He hit it over the net and Kurt returned it.

The ball zoomed past Sophie. Too late, she dove and landed in the sand.

"Get in the game, Soph!" Marty yelled.

"Okay, okay," she snipped back.

Since running into Noah at their lighthouse a couple days ago, she hadn't once seen him out and about. She hadn't noticed him in his yard or on the porch, in town or at the beach. The house shades were still closed. It didn't matter the time of day or night, the house looked the same. Shades drawn. No lights flickering from within.

She'd thought Noah staying out of her way would ease her mind. Instead his vanishing act had set in motion a different set of worries. What if he did develop PTSD? What if her wish had come true and he'd drunk himself to death out at the lighthouse?

"You guys bombed!" Kurt heckled.

The kids—and Marty, for that matter—had been hooting and hollering at every point they earned. "Your serve." Marty tossed Lauren the ball. "Let's see what you can do, *munchkin.*"

Lauren glared at Marty. She hated that baby nickname.

"Right here, munchkin, right here!" Marty yelled, clapping his hands together.

"You're toast, Uncle Marty." Lauren grinned. She stepped back to the serving line, her face set with concentration. Tossing the ball into the air, she whacked it over the net. Marty popped the ball up, right above Sophie. Sophie jumped, planning to tip the ball over the net, and miscalculated the angle. The ball hit the ground by her feet.

"Woo-hoo!" The kids screamed triumphantly.

"I want a rematch!" Marty said.

"You're on," Kurt yelled.

"Tomorrow," Marty said.

"Now or never," Lauren challenged.

"No can do, munchkin," Marty explained. "I promised Brittany I'd take her to the mainland to check out the casino we're taking everyone to next week."

The casino on the mainland? This was the first Sophie had heard of an excursion off Mirabelle as being part of the wedding festivities.

"Oh, good excuse, Uncle Marty," Kurt teased, running off to join Lauren.

"Tomorrow, you guys are going down!" Marty yelled before

joining Brittany on the sidelines. "You should have played," he said to her. "We needed you."

"Are you kidding? Volleyball would so ruin my nails." Brittany wrapped her arm around Marty's waist.

"You want to come to the casino with us, Soph?" Marty asked.

"Nah, I don't think so." Sophie didn't do spur-of-the-moment jaunts off the island.

"Oh, come on," Brittany urged. "It'll be fun."

Leaving Mirabelle was never Sophie's idea of fun. It'd been almost a year since the last time she'd gone to the mainland for a back-to-school shopping trip with the kids. Just the idea of getting into a car and driving down a highway at fifty-five miles an hour made her heart race.

It hadn't always been this way. When she'd been young, Sophie had loved heading off into the outside world, but then her dad had died and she'd taken over running the inn. One thing had led to another and before she'd realized it, years had gone by without going to the mainland. Now the only time Sophie ever left Mirabelle was after—and *only* after—weeks of advance planning, giving herself time to mentally prepare for stepping into the outside world. Necessity had somehow turned to a quiet acceptance.

"You sure you don't want to come?" Marty asked.

"Positive," Sophie said. "You guys have fun." As they walked away, she called out, "Hey, Marty?"

He spun around. "Yeah?"

"Have you seen Noah at all?"

"No." Frowning, he shook his head. "I went up to his house both yesterday and today to visit and drop off a wedding invitation."

"And?"

"He never answered the door."

Sophie glanced up the hill. *You've always been our responsible one,* she could hear her parents' voices. *Well, Noah is not my responsibility. Not. Not. Not.*

The sooner he left this island, the better. For everyone.

NOAH STOOD BACK FROM the sheer curtains covering the front picture window and looked down the hill. From here he could see miles of the Mirabelle shoreline and, out ahead, the seemingly endless expanse of Lake Superior.

A white latticed gazebo near the point heralded the beginning of the Rousseau property line and beyond that, a great meandering lawn leading to the Mirabelle Island Inn's sprawling veranda. Bookended with columned turrets and painted pristine white with a red tiled roof, the inn looked exactly as he remembered it, although the trees had grown, obscuring some of the property.

The back lawn of Mirabelle Island Inn, though, he could see as clear as a bell. People were playing croquet and horseshoes. He picked Sophie out at the volleyball net on the beach within seconds. Even if he'd wanted to—which he didn't—there wasn't much of a chance he'd be joining that crew. For the last several days, he hadn't slept for more than a few hours a shot, and he couldn't remember the last time he'd been able to hold down more than a mouthful or two of food. He was a mess and he sure as hell didn't want to bring everyone else down.

He tore his gaze away from the window and glanced half-heartedly at the supplies—scrapers, brushes, primer and paint—he'd had delivered from the hardware store. For two days he'd been planning on getting outside and working on the house, and for two days he'd been coming up with excuses to stay inside. It was too hot, too cold, too cloudy, too sunny. Today the excuse was needing to get back to work on his book.

He sat at his grandmother's dining room table and stared at his laptop screen. The file with his manuscript about his stint in Iraq sat there, awaiting a word or two or thirty thousand. No matter what he did, or didn't do, he couldn't seem to string a sentence together to save his soul, and he couldn't motivate himself to care one way or the other. Not only hadn't he finished the damn thing, he'd yet to sort through his myriad files of photos to be included within the finished book.

He hated feeling this way and had no idea what to do to get back some semblance of normalcy, but it was becoming apparent that his doctors had been wrong. He'd been wrong. Coming to Mirabelle had been a mistake. He'd been blissful in his ignorance with regard to Isaac's death, and being near Sophie was far worse than not thinking about her at all these many years.

Sophie. He had a momentary thought of sending her a message. An SOS. Sail a paper airplane down the hill. Leave a window blind at a certain angle. Position rocks in particular patterns along the cobblestone road. Who needed cell phones or text messaging? He and Sophie, grounded or not, had always seemed to get through to each other when they'd needed each other the most.

Oh, Soph. Did you ever really love me?

That question had run through his mind many times through the years and he never came any closer to an answer, or maybe the answer was one he had a hard time accepting. He'd left and she'd married Isaac. Didn't that say it all?

More than once he'd wondered if Isaac had always had a thing for Sophie. Though Noah's brother had consistently denied any attraction, the summer Isaac graduated from college and returned home a full-fledged man was the same summer Sophie had bloomed into a woman. A man would have to have been blind not to notice, and it's not as if there had been a lot of options on the island.

What would've happened if Noah had stayed on Mirabelle? She would've had to choose between the two of them, and Noah had a feeling she wouldn't have chosen him.

The cursor stared at him from his laptop.

Start anywhere. The point was to start.

Tomorrow. He'd do it tomorrow. Noah dragged himself out of his chair and a jolt of pain, as if someone had suddenly pressed a live electrical wire to his knee, shot through his leg, making him stumble and nearly fall. *Damned phantom pains!* He flopped onto the couch, pulled off his prosthetic and threw it across the room. It crashed against the wall, making a satisfying hole.

"Sorry, Grandma. This isn't like me, I know. I'm not sure I'll ever be *me* again."

Coming back to Mirabelle had been the second biggest mistake of his life. He reached for another bottle of booze he never should've had delivered, but then drowning his pain had to be better than wallowing in it.

"GOOD AFTERNOON, ARLO," Sophie said as the horse-drawn carriage passed her along Island Drive. After having started work quite early that morning, she'd decided to head to town before dinnertime for a few groceries. Only light, fluffy clouds dotted the clear blue sky and there was enough of a breeze to keep the gnats away.

"Ayep." Arlo nodded back. "That it is, Sophie."

The moment, in fact, would've been perfect, except that Arlo was only transporting a single couple from the ferry to their lodging destination. In Mirabelle's heyday, his carriage as well as at least three more would've been loaded to the gills with guests and their luggage. Those booming business days were gone and didn't look to be coming back any time soon.

Sophie's family had weathered these kinds of slow times before, so the inn would be all right, but she wasn't sure about some of the other establishments on the island. Resolving to bring up the issue with the town council after Marty's wedding, Sophie continued her walk toward Main Street. She glanced up Bennett Hill.

As far as she knew, Noah hadn't emerged from his grandmother's house since the night she'd seen him at the lighthouse. With the blinds and curtains still drawn and no outside activity, the place looked as desolate today as it had before he arrived. He seemed to be taking his promise to stay out of her way to an extreme. Maybe he was in tougher shape than he'd looked. Then again, maybe it was none of her business.

She put Noah firmly out of her mind and continued on to Newman's grocery store. Dan Newman, the owner, was putting out fresh produce on a display as she walked through the entrance. "Hello there, Sophie."

"Hi, Dan."

She put a few oranges in her basket and before she could stop herself asked, "Dan, have you seen Noah Bennett at all?"

"Yeah, I heard he was on the island."

"Have you seen him? Here. In your store?" This was, after all, the only place to buy groceries on the island.

He pursed his lips. "Nope. Can't say that I have."

"He hasn't bought any food?"

"Well, he did call here the other day to have some things delivered. Strange, though."

"What?"

"We were out of a few things he'd ordered. When our delivery boy took them up later on, he said the other bags were still on the porch."

"Did you call? Make sure Noah was okay?"

"It's really none of my business, Sophie."

"None of your—"

Since when had that ever stopped anyone on this island from helping another resident? Except that Noah, from the time he'd turned into an obstinate teenager, had been treated as more of an outsider than an islander, and somehow she'd let herself fall right into step with them.

She debated, get involved or stay out of it? Either course held its own pitfalls, but there was only one way to get Noah off her island and out of her life before he turned her world upside down. All over again.

After grabbing some staples, she rushed out the door. By the time she reached Grandma Bennett's front steps, she was out of breath. The grocery bags were no longer on the porch, but there was no sign of life inside.

She rang the doorbell. Nothing. Pounded on the door. Still nothing. The door was locked. "Noah!" she yelled and then listened for any answering sounds. She pounded again. "Dammit, Noah, are you in there?"

"Go away." Although the voice coming from inside the house was muffled, there was no doubt it was Noah.

"Open the door!"

He wasn't moving around in there.

If memory served, Grandma Bennett had always kept an extra key under a rock by the garden hose in the back. Sophie ran around the corner of the house, found the old key nearly buried under years of decaying leaves and debris, and let herself in through the kitchen.

Despite being sunny and seventy-five degrees outside, the house was dark and had a dank feel. "Noah?"

"Dammit, Sophie. Go away."

She found him in the living room, lying on the couch,

looking as if he hadn't shaved in a month. He was wearing shorts, making the fact that he wasn't wearing his prosthetic immediately apparent. The vision of his leg cut off just below his knee made her throat close with emotion, but then she noticed the empty bottle of tequila on the floor by the coffee table. "Are you drunk?"

"Why do you care?"

"I don't."

He put his hands on either side of his head as if holding it together. "Go away. I don't want you here." He was pale, thin and obviously waking up from a long and drawn-out binge.

"You've got a hangover."

"Yeah. So?"

"Well, this is great. Perfect." Disgusted, she shook her head. "This is how you go about getting better, huh?"

He didn't answer.

"I don't know how you lost your leg and, honestly, I don't care. But you're alive. Get off your ass and quit feeling sorry for yourself."

His angry gaze settled on her face. "Who the hell do you think you are?"

Good. His antagonism was good. She could deal with him just fine when he was like this. "Apparently, the only person on this island who gives a damn whether you live or die."

He rolled away. Wouldn't look at her.

"Poor Noah," Sophie said. "Got his foot blown off and now his life is over."

"Screw you."

"Wouldn't you like to try."

"Maybe I would." For a moment, he glared at her, looking for all the world as if he might be furious enough to make good on the threat. "Go away, Sophie."

Ignoring him, she glanced around expecting to find dirty dishes and opened bags of food scattered around the house. Instead, there was only the clutter of newspapers, magazines and, of all things, a handgun lying on the coffee table. His prosthetic lay on the floor below a nice big hole in the wall. It certainly looked as if what he'd said the other night at the lighthouse was true. He wasn't eating, and he wasn't sleeping. He was angry and frustrated and taking it out on his grandmother's house and himself.

She had to admit, though, the gun bothered her more than anything. "What's the gun for?"

"Nothing. It's what happens when you hang with the military as much as I have."

"That's a lie if I've ever heard one."

"It's none of your damned business."

Anger, red-hot and piercing, surged inside her. "Well, why don't you just pick it up then, and put yourself out of your misery."

"Trust me. I've thought about it."

This was not the Noah she'd known most of her life. Where was the young boy with the mischievous smirk? The young man who could beat anyone around the island in a kayak? The man whose passion for life had come through in every one of his articles and books? Yes, she'd read them. Every single one. This was not the man who, over the years, had exposed political issues and brought to light famine and genocide all over the world.

If he kept on like this, he would end up being on Mirabelle for months, years even. There was no way she was living with that, not if she had anything to say about it. She picked up the phone and dialed.

CHAPTER SIX

"MIRABELLE ISLAND INN," Jan said, her voice clear and pleasant as she answered Sophie's phone call.

"Jan, it's Sophie. If anyone's looking for me," she said, walking into the kitchen and loading the few dirty dishes into the dishwasher, "I'm going to be gone for a little while, okay?"

"Oh, no, you're not!" Noah yelled, sitting up.

Sophie ignored him and started the cleaning cycle.

"Sure. Everything's under control," Jan said. "Are you all right?"

"I'm fine." She rummaged through the groceries, still sitting in bags on the kitchen counter and took out a can of soup. "Can you check in with the kids and have them call my cell if they need me?"

"Go away, Sophie!" Noah was putting on his leg.

"No problem," Jan said, hesitant. "Where are you? Who's yelling in the background?"

Sophie dumped the soup into a pan and set it to warming on the stove top. "If there's an emergency, I'll be at Grandma Bennett's."

"No, you won't," Noah muttered.

A short pause hung over the phone line before Jan said, "Sophie, you may have forgotten, but I remember very clearly what you went through after Noah left. I don't think I had a dry shoulder for months—"

"Trust me, Jan, I remember. This is no big deal."

"Listen to her, Soph," he mumbled, standing and heading toward the kitchen. "You shouldn't be here."

Another pause on the phone line. "When will you be home?"

"In a couple hours," Sophie said.

"All right. I'll take care of everything."

Sophie hung up, sidestepped past a very angry Noah and ran upstairs, stripped the sheets off the bed he'd obviously been tossing and turning in and snapped up a towel from the bathroom floor. She went back downstairs and threw the linens in the washing machine. When she turned around, Noah was standing in the laundry room doorway, blocking her exit.

The young Noah she remembered was gone and in his place was a man. An angry, sullen, brooding man. Broad shouldered and built. Though his hospital stay had likely set him back a bit, he was still an intimidating presence. Physical awareness zapped her hard and fast. This laundry room was much too small for the two of them.

"I don't want you here," he snapped.

"Too bad." She pushed past him, went into the kitchen and checked the soup. It'd do. She dumped the contents of the pan into a bowl, smacked the bowl onto the table and stepped back, setting her hands on her hips. Who knew when he'd last taken any food. "Sit," she said. "Eat."

He didn't budge. Then he grimaced as if in pain and his shoulders sagged. "Just go, Sophie. Please." He leaned against the doorway, taking his weight off his left leg.

"No," she said. "Not until you eat something."

"If it makes you feel any better," he muttered, looking away, "I still can't hold anything down."

"If you want me gone, you'll have to try."

Without a word, he dropped onto the chair and shoved three spoonfuls of soup into his mouth.

"More," she said.

"You want me to throw up? Are you getting some kind of sick pleasure out of this?"

"Maybe I am." She opened a package of saltine crackers and tossed it onto the table next to him. "These should settle your stomach."

She glanced into his eyes, saw the flash of heat there and felt an instantaneous response. *Traitor.*

But then what did she expect? For most of their childhood, Noah had been like a brother to Sophie and then almost overnight, her hormones had kicked in and changed everything between them. She hadn't been able to stop watching his lips, had been obsessed with wanting to find out what it would be like to kiss, not just any boy, but Noah. Only Noah.

It had taken him a while to catch up to her hormone-laden train of thoughts. When he finally did, they hadn't been able to keep their hands off each other. By the time they were in tenth grade they were secretly necking during recess, after school and every other chance they got to be alone. Sophie and Noah. Noah and Sophie. Hand in hand. Arm in arm. Until they'd gotten caught sneaking off to a janitorial closet during a school-wide assembly and the principal had been forced to call their parents.

From then on, their freedom had been gone, but the separation, the constant monitoring, only made the times they'd managed to be alone together all the more special. They'd been forced to get sneaky. By the time they were seniors in high school, they had their routines down pat. They'd planned times when they were sure they could be alone, like when their parents were neck-deep in tourists. With blankets, lanterns and food and drinks in coolers, they'd snuck away on kayaks or sailboats to the other uninhabited islands. Where no one could find them. Where no one could interrupt. Where exploring sex had turned into making love.

Oh, no. You are not going there. Get done what you need to and get the hell out of here.

She stalked into the living room, drew back the curtains and opened the blinds, letting the afternoon sun blaze inside. By the time she'd propped open the front door and gone back to the kitchen, Noah was taking the last spoonful of soup.

"Now." She leveled her gaze on him, ready for an argument. "When's the last time you got any exercise or at least some fresh air?"

His answering chuckle held absolutely no humor. "Sophie, I'm not a child."

"Then quit acting like one."

"I understand what you're trying to do, and there's no point."

"You came here to get better, right? Well, it's not going to happen all on its own."

"Why?" He slammed his spoon onto the table and stared at her. "Why do you care?"

"I don't!" she yelled back.

"Then why are you doing this?"

"Because as long as you're sitting around feeling sorry for yourself you won't be getting better." He'd be disrupting her thoughts, her life. She couldn't let him disrupt Kurt's and Lauren's lives. She put her hands on her hips and met his gaze. "I want you the hell off my island! The sooner, the better."

GET HIM BETTER SO HE COULD leave Mirabelle. Now *that* made sense to Noah, but there was no way he was spending any more time around Sophie than absolutely necessary. God help them both if either one of them started caring for the other again.

"You need to leave." He pushed himself up from the table and hobbled back to the sofa in the living room. He'd no sooner sat down than pain ripped through his body. He stiffened and closed his eyes, letting short bursts of air puff out from between his lips.

"Noah," she said, "what's happening?"

"Phantom pains," he grunted. "Feels like an electrical shock zapping my leg."

"Can I do anything?"

"No," he bit out. "It'll pass."

"There's no medication for that?" she asked.

"Painkillers don't do a thing." He waved a hand at the prescription bottles sitting on the coffee table. "Believe me, I've tried every pill under the sun."

"Physical therapy?"

The worst of the pain subsided and he ran his hands over his face. "They've been trying something new with mirrors that they say makes a difference." He motioned toward a full-length mirror leaning against the wall. "But it sounds like a bunch of hooey to me."

"You should be trying anything and everything to get better."

"I should, huh? What do you know?" Who the hell did she think she was? Florence Freaking Nightingale? "You have no clue what I'm going through."

"You need—"

"What I need is for you to leave!"

"I'm not—"

"Get the fuck out of here, Sophie! Now!"

She stepped back as if he'd hit her. "What happened to the Noah I knew?"

"Long gone, Sophie, and he won't ever be coming back."

"You're pathetic. You know that?" Rousing, she charged into the kitchen and came back carrying an unopened bottle of whiskey. Slamming the bottle down on the coffee table, she said, "There you go, Noah. Knock yourself out." Then she left.

The door slammed and Noah cringed as the noise reverberated in his head. Thank God she was gone. Blissful silence settled over his grandmother's house as he stared at the whiskey. *Why the hell not?* Reaching for the bottle, he barely managed to crack it open. *Pathetic? Hell, yes.* Sophie had always known him better than anyone else.

THE NEXT DAY, SOPHIE POUNDED on Grandma Bennett's front door sometime in the late afternoon. When Noah, all but passed out on the living room sofa, didn't answer, she let herself in, apparently having kept his grandmother's spare house key. Without a word, she made him more soup, carried it into the living room along with a banana and announced, "I'm not leaving until that food is gone."

Noah glared at her for a few minutes, but then caved, his stomach feeling like an empty pit. The moment he finished his last bite, she took off out the front door without another word.

They went through the same charade the next day and the next. Each time, she added more food items and meatier portions, but never said anything. On the fifth day, she brought a meal from the inn. The moment she opened the take-out container, the smells of Josie's beef Stroganoff hit his senses and his stomach growled with hunger.

Like it or not, her tactic was working. He hadn't swallowed a drop of liquor in two days. He was sleeping marginally better and his metabolism was giving it a good go, forcing him to have to supplement the meals she'd been bringing him.

She held out the food. "So are you up for a walk today?"

"I don't need your help. I can do this on my own."

"What you need is some fresh air."

"When did you get to be such a know-it-all busybody?"

"When haven't I been?"

Sick of playing her game, he took the container out of her hand and ate.

When he'd finished, she asked, "How's the food settling in your stomach?"

"So far, so good."

"Then let's go for a walk."

"You mean go for a limp? Not interested, Nurse Ratched."

"Are you sleeping at night?"

"No."

"Lack of exercise isn't helping." She crossed her arms. "Noah, come on. Let's go."

Get him better so he could leave Mirabelle.

He did need to leave this island, for his dad, for himself. For Sophie. He needed to get off his ass and put the pieces of his life back together. "Okay, I give." Too tired to fight anymore, he followed her out onto the porch.

They set off down the hill, and for a long while he and Sophie walked side by side in complete silence. Anger hung heavy in the air between them. What did you say to a woman who'd been your best friend and most passionate lover all rolled into one? A woman who'd married your own brother, for God's sake. Nothing, that's what.

After a time, he realized they'd struck out on the same roads, in the same direction they used to walk. How could she have stood it all these years? "Don't you ever get sick of it? The same paths over and over and over."

She glanced sideways at him, looking as if she might not answer him. "Every once in a while," she finally said. "But there's a…comfort in it, too. In the stability."

"In the boredom."

"You say tomato," she said. "Bright lights and big cities don't necessarily lead to a more fulfilling life. If you ask me, those always hunting for the latest war zones are the ones with issues."

"Touché."

"Does your leg hurt?" she asked.

"A little." As weak as he'd gotten from lying in bed during his extended hospital stay, he felt every bit an invalid walking next to Sophie.

"Maybe you need a new leg."

"I've got one up at the house. The new foot's supposed to be good for all kinds of activity. Walking, running. Hell, even skating."

"Then why do you wear this one?"

"I guess I've gotten used to it. This is the temporary leg they gave me after the surgery, and I suppose I'm a little attached to it."

"But you're limping. Don't you think the new leg will fit better?"

He didn't know what to say, didn't know how to explain his jumbled-up emotions.

"What are you worried about, Noah?"

"Worried?" He stopped. "You don't know me anymore, Sophie. Don't presume to know what I'd be worried about."

They walked along in virtual silence for close to an hour, making a big circle around the island. He had to admit it felt good to be outside, sunshine hitting his face, fresh air in his lungs, the sounds of robins and chickadees chirping nearby. When they came to the Rousseau woods, they both turned onto the path they'd always taken as kids, leading right by an old gnarly oak that had been great for climbing and hiding behind for stolen kisses.

"You still running?" he asked, redirecting his thoughts.

"Most mornings."

"You can run all you want," he mused. "You still can't run yourself off this island."

She glared at him.

"I know, I know. I say tomato." He tried to shake his thoughts clear. "Same route?"

"That we used to run? No." She shook her head. "These days, I take the road up, come back through the state forest and finish through here." She pointed toward a path running along the shore, but Noah didn't bother looking in that direction.

He couldn't seem to take his eyes off Sophie's face. Her skin was dappled with sunlight streaming through the forest canopy. It was amazing how little she'd aged. She seemed more petite somehow, but that probably had more to do with him having grown than anything. Surrounded as she was by leaves, grasses and brush the green in her eyes was more pronounced. She looked like a wood nymph, one of the fairies some of the old people swore inhabited the quietest parts of Mirabelle.

She caught his gaze and the moment became awkward. He turned away too quickly, hit the trunk of the tree with his bad knee and pain zinged up his side. "Shit!" He grimaced, leaned back against the tree and rubbed his leg.

"How'd it happen?" she asked quietly, as if she wasn't sure it was her place. "Losing your foot?"

In the hospital, Noah had briefly described the explosion to various military personnel in order for them to file their reports, but, since then, he'd tried not to think about it. "It was exactly like you see in the movies. I'd been with the same unit for a couple months. They were acting on a tip about a small cell of insurgents hiding in Mosul.

"Out of nowhere, a roadside bomb hit our truck. It was probably remotely controlled, and they were waiting for us. I was in the rear with Mick, my military guide. When the bomb hit, I felt a burning sensation on the back of my left leg and was thrown out of the truck. Lost my foot, broke an arm and a few ribs, concussion, shrapnel punctures." He touched his chest and arms where shrapnel had hit him. "My back felt like it was on fire."

"The others?"

He grew silent, remembering. "Everyone else was killed."

The sound of Sophie's sharp intake of breath hit him hard. "I'm so sorry, Noah."

"For me? Losing a foot is nothing."

"It changed your life."

Curiously, for the first time since the bombing he wanted to talk, but not to just anyone. He wanted to spill his guts to Sophie, tell her everything that had happened over the years, his failures and successes, how his brushes with death and seeing others die had changed him.

"What about John?" he said, angry, not at Sophie, but at life. "He was a month from heading home after three tours of duty and never got the chance to hold his new baby daughter. Or Lindsey. She'd been in Iraq only two months, wanting to follow in the footsteps of her three brothers who all made it out of there alive. Then there's Mick, Chris, Leon. What about them?" There was nothing she could say, and he felt bad for lashing out at her. "I'm sorry."

"You've seen some terrible things. Things I can only imagine."

"I used to keep a journal of all the people I'd known who'd died in all the wars, military actions or peacekeeping operations I've been involved in through the years. During Iraq, I gave up."

"Too many?"

"Let's say I know more than I'd like about putting on field dressings."

"Why'd you keep doing it?"

"I was afraid no one would write about all the things the world needed to know. Half of what I've written has never seen the light of day because there isn't a newspaper or publisher out there who'll touch it."

"Why do you care?"

He'd never thought about it before. "I suppose I knew early on I could never be a cop, or a soldier."

"Too much like your dad."

He nodded. "Guess, in my own way, I'm always looking for justice, for the truth."

Somehow, someway, the anger that had insulated and protected each of them seemed to have dimmed, and the awkwardness between them reared up again. Suddenly, he was done talking and done walking. "I need to go back," he said.

"Get some sleep. I'll stop by again tomorrow after work."

"Don't, Sophie, please." He turned and went up the hill alone. She was hell on his nerves. "I'll get myself off this damned island."

CHAPTER SEVEN

WITH THE SUN BARELY RISING over the treetops off the east side of the island, Jim Bennett slowly motored his boat into the Mirabelle marina and aimed for his slip. He'd come in and out of this maze of docks so many times in the past forty years he could probably make the trip blindfolded. Good thing, too, as his mind was nowhere near the task at hand.

He docked his thirty-footer and took the pipe out of his mouth. After tying down the boat, he gutted the whitefish and salmon he'd caught that morning and threw them on ice. Gulls cawed overhead, piercing the quiet morning air in their quest for breakfast. He tossed the fish entrails in the water, letting the noisy buzzards fight over them, and washed his hands.

"You got in late this morning."

Jim barely heard the soft feminine voice over the sound of the gulls squabbling. He glanced up to find Josie standing on the dock holding a take-out container.

"I brought you some breakfast," she said.

He held out his hand, helping her climb onto the boat. "I thought we agreed to meet at the inn in the mornings."

"You hungry or not?"

"All right. All right. I just don't like people talking."

"They're going to talk, anyway," Josie said. "No matter what you and I do."

"Yeah, well, I don't like stirring the pot."

"You know, when we first started seeing each other, I understood your privacy issues. But now…" She hesitated. "I'm not Gloria, Jim."

"You think I don't know that?"

"Sometimes I wonder."

He poured her the last cup of coffee from his thermos. "It should still be hot." He held it out for her.

"You go ahead." She sat across from him. "I've had enough already this morning."

He opened the container she'd brought to find scrambled eggs and ham along with some hash browns, all still hot. "Caught a couple nice ones this morning, if you can use 'em." He tapped the cooler with the tip of his tennis shoe. The position of police chief on Mirabelle didn't pay all that much and left him with more free time than he liked, so he ran a small charter fishing operation and sold fish to the restaurants on the island. "If the inn can't use 'em, I'll take 'em to Delores."

"Marty asked if we could do an old-fashioned fish fry one night when all his guests are here, so we'll take them."

"How's the first week of summer season going?"

"Oh, the usual. Jan set up the wrong room for a buffet the other afternoon, and then changed the time for lunch yesterday and forgot to tell me. Nothing catastrophic."

"You ready for Marty's wedding party?"

"Not yet, but we'll get through it."

"You always do." He finished the last of the breakfast, sat back and stuffed tobacco into his pipe.

"Well, I gotta get back to work." Josie took the take-out container and gave him a goodbye peck on the cheek.

Jim glanced around the marina and breathed a sigh of relief

that the docks were still deserted. He held out his hand and helped her out of the boat.

She paused, as if debating something.

"What?" he asked.

"Jan was complaining that Sophie's been spending a lot of time with Noah."

The news seemed to cause a tight feeling in his chest. "When? Where were they?"

"Every day this week. At your mom's house most of the time. Arlo said they walked by the stables last night."

Son of a...

"Jim, what if you've been wrong about them all these years?"

"You don't know Noah the way I do."

"Well, I know Sophie, and I know she's a good judge of character."

"Humph," he grunted. "Growing up on this island, she's too naive for her own good."

"You need to tell him—and her—the truth."

"I'm not telling anyone anything." He threw her a questioning glance.

"Don't look at me." She headed down the dock. "Everyone's chickens have a way of coming home to roost all on their own."

ON SUNDAY MORNING, MORE THAN a week after he'd first arrived on Mirabelle, Noah awoke, or rather slid out of bed as there had been very little actual sleep involved, before the sun had risen. Feeling damned near close to human for the first time in a long while, he brewed himself some coffee and toasted a piece of bread and then sat at the table with his laptop in front of him.

After opening his work-in-process he forced out a couple words. He typed a line and deleted it. Typed another few and deleted those, too. Over and over, he attempted to pick up where he'd left off on his documentary on the Iraqi war and over and over, he hit a dead end. He was about ready to fling the damned computer across the room when the paragraph he'd written before the explosion caught his eye.

He backed up and read more. The thoughts and words flowed like the current on a river, smoothly, quickly, and, almost as if the man who'd written those passages was gone, he didn't recognize a single line as his own. Would that man ever come back? Not with, for all intents and purposes, a gun pointed at his head that was for sure.

After forcing down the toast, he pushed away from the table and grabbed that full-length mirror his doctors had ordered him to use for therapy against the phantom pains. The first day he'd been here, the delivery boy had set it against the wall by the front door and that's exactly where it had stood ever since.

His doctors had told him that phantom pain, while very real in a physical sense, could be the result of mixed messages being sent by the brain to the nerves. The experimental treatment they had him try in the hospital required him to sit with his legs flat in front of him and a full-length mirror, lying horizontally between his legs, standing upright on its long edge with the reflective side facing his good, full leg. While watching the mirror he was to flex and move his leg, supposedly tricking his brain into thinking he had two good legs. Maybe it was time to give it a shot again.

Noah sat lengthwise on the couch in his grandmother's living room, his legs, such as they were, stretched in front of him. Then he set the mirror between his legs and rotated his right foot and flexed and released, all the while watching the reflection in the mirror. He repeated the process as many times as he could stand.

It looked as if he had two good legs, and if he concentrated he could almost—almost—remember what it felt like to run, to walk without discomfort. To be whole. As much as he wanted to, he refused to glance at the other side of the mirror at his stump. It was nothing more than a mass of scar tissue. No, he wasn't close to whole. Never would be again.

He moved the mirror, set it against the wall near the box holding his new prosthetic. Maybe Sophie was right. Maybe he *was* worried about changing the status quo. If he got better, recovered one hundred percent, then he'd have to get back to life. Full swing. Then he'd have no reason for not writing his book. The old leg reminded him he was a cripple, told the world to back off. He was damaged goods. He had an excuse for hiding away. A new leg left him no excuse for being afraid.

He flipped back the box cover and stared at the high-tech piece of machinery. Made of the most advanced materials available, the leg was at least ten pounds lighter than his temporary one. Carbon fiber with an arched foot, it would no doubt feel unbelievably better at the end of what was left of his leg.

What are you worried about, Noah?

That it'll be time to leave Mirabelle.

He closed the box. He wasn't ready.

In the meantime, he surely could keep busy. He gathered some supplies and headed outside. It was tough. He hadn't wanted to get moving or leave the safe confines of his grandmother's house, but he did get immense satisfaction from having trimmed every shrub in the entire one acre lot and scraped and primed all except a small section of the entire back side of the cottage before Sophie showed up late that afternoon.

"The yard looks good," he heard her say.

"Thanks." He looked down at her from his position near the top of the steel ladder.

"Marty's wedding guests have been arriving all day, so I wasn't going to come up. But then Josie made a big batch of lemonade and I knew you've been out here working all day." She held up a large plastic pitcher. "Would you like to take a break?"

He glanced down at her. *She just wants you off her island. That's all.* He wiped the sweat off his forehead. "Give me a few more minutes and I'll be finished painting the back." And very likely finished for the day as this was the first time he'd done any kind of manual labor since losing his foot.

"I'll be right out." She disappeared through the back door of the house.

When she came outside a little while later holding two glasses filled with ice and lemonade, he was washing his hands with the hose. After he'd finished, she held out a glass.

"Thank you." He took a sip. It tasted so refreshing that he downed the glass and poured himself another. Then he sat on the back stoop in the cooler shade.

"Did you sleep last night?"

"You mean that thing people are supposed to do at night?" He chuckled. "No."

"Have you eaten anything today?"

"Sure."

"Noah—"

"Mom!" Kurt's shout came through the front-door screen and out the back.

"I told you, she's not in there," Lauren said.

"I'm in back," Sophie yelled.

Only seconds later, the twins came running around the corner of the house.

"What are you two doing?" Sophie asked.

"Jan told us to come and get you," Kurt said.

"Smart woman that Jan," Noah whispered.

"And," Lauren said, holding out a container, "Josie made Noah some dinner."

"Well, wasn't that nice." Noah accepted the container.

"Will you be able to eat it?"

"Actually," he said, holding Sophie's gaze. "I'm starving."

"Roasted chicken, mixed vegetables and mashed potatoes and gravy," Lauren said. "I cut you a piece of the mixed berry pie I made myself."

"You did?"

"Mmm-hmm." She nodded.

"Making pies by yourself." He studied her. "How old are you?"

"Fourteen," she said. "But everyone says we're mature for our age."

Kids. Always in such a hurry to grow up. "Well, thank you, Lauren," Noah said. "Is this what you had for dinner?"

Lauren nodded.

"I rarely cook," Sophie said. "That's one benefit to having a trained gourmet in the kitchen."

"I'm surprised you've stayed so trim."

Kurt frowned at him as if he sensed there was something between Noah and his mother and didn't like it one bit. The feeling was mutual.

"Let's go." Kurt tugged on Sophie's hand. "Marty said he wants you to come back down for the fire."

"Are you coming to the bonfire, Noah?" Lauren asked.

"I'm not so sure—"

"Please come," Lauren urged. "You're family, remember?" She looked to her mom for support.

"Marty would love to visit with you," Sophie said, standing next to Kurt.

"We'll see."

Kurt walked away and down the hill. "Come on!"

"Chill!" Lauren said, following him.

Noah followed the three of them around the side of the house and watched their downhill progress. Sophie. A mom. With kids and a business, she was obviously entrenched on this island. And him? He'd be leaving as soon as he could sleep through the night and hold down three square meals.

Nothing had changed.

BY SUNDAY NIGHT, MOST of the wedding guests, including Marty and Sophie's two sisters and their families, had arrived. True to their word, Jan, Sarah and Josie were taking care of everything. They'd prepped rooms, registered guests, set up buffets in the main dining hall for every meal, and distributed room keys and maps of the island as well as the week's calendar of events.

Sophie continued to check in with them from time to time, but for the most part, she was free to do as she pleased. Even Lauren and Kurt needed barely any supervision once their cousins had arrived. This island was their personal playground, and they loved showing their cousins around. It was the only time Lauren, in particular, appreciated living on Mirabelle.

At dusk, while Brittany set up extra chairs, Sophie built a fire in the large, stone-encircled pit and the kids chased fireflies around the inn's expansive back lawn. Once she'd gotten the campfire going, she sat in a folding camp chair and looked into the sky.

"Hey, kids," Brittany yelled. "Go find some marshmallow roasting sticks. Get one for me, too, while you're at it."

They dashed off and returned only minutes later, huddling in a circle. The campfire blazed, its flames leaping into the midnight-blue sky and casting flickering yellow-orange light onto the faces of Lauren, Kurt and Brittany, as well as several other nieces and nephews of Sophie's. Groups of guests and relatives milled about, some by the shoreline, some near the fire, and others near the picnic table Jan had set up with the makings for s'mores.

Sophie leaned back in her chair and zipped her jacket. Though the temperature was mild for this early in summer, an occasional chilly breeze blew in off the lake, making the heat emanating from the fire all the more comforting.

"This is going to be a perfect marshmallow roasting stick," Kurt said, continuing to strip the bark off a green branch with his pocketknife. "Want me to do yours?" he asked Lauren.

"Sure." Absently, Lauren handed Kurt the branch and went back to poking the red-hot coals at the center of the fire with a stick.

Sophie studied her son's profile. Tonight more than usual, she could see Noah in his features. The Bennett brothers had looked alike in some ways, but had been so different in personality.

Both brothers had been determined and achievement-oriented, but Isaac had been duty bound and methodical in his approach toward life. He'd been cautious and rarely failed at anything he set out to accomplish. In fact, Isaac had always been so meticulous Sophie had never imagined he'd be killed in the line of duty. Guess there was no accounting for stray bullets.

Noah, on the other hand, had never been frightened of failure. He'd enjoyed the rush that came from taking chances. Always, he'd pushed his boundaries. She supposed that's what drew her to him when they'd been younger. He'd never been afraid to do anything, to go anywhere. So much like Lauren and Kurt. Or was she imagining that connection?

She shook her head, clearing her thoughts. "I wonder what's keeping Marty," she said.

"It looks like he's visiting with someone," Brittany said,

more subdued than normal as she lost herself in the fire. "He'll be back in a minute." The flames seemed to mesmerize her. "Marty said he wants to have a fire every night, even in the winter, after we move—" She stopped, tucking her chin into the neck of her jacket.

Sophie glanced across the flames.

Kurt's jaw dropped. "You and Marty are moving to Mirabelle?"

CHAPTER EIGHT

"WHAT?" LAUREN LOOKED UP from the fire. "You're going to be living here? On Mirabelle?"

"I wasn't supposed to say anything," Brittany said, meeting Sophie's eyes with a worried expression. "Not until Marty talked with you, Sophie."

"Are you kidding?" Sophie said. "We'll be excited to have you!"

"Where are you going to live?" Lauren asked. "I hope you're close so we can see each other every day."

"We'd like to build a hotel," Brittany said, sitting straighter in her chair, and Sophie felt prickles of concern run up her spine.

"You should put it right there." Lauren pointed to the Rousseau forest west of the inn. "Neighbors would be so cool!"

"That's what we thought!" Brittany caught the buzz of the kids' infectious excitement.

"Tight!" Kurt's eyes went wide.

The trust land? Sophie's concern turned into full-fledged alarm. That land held the only virgin forest on the entire island. This was the forest Sophie had built forts in and tramped through as a kid. The forest where she and Noah had shared first kisses.

"What kind of hotel?" Lauren asked, leaning forward expectantly.

"A big one!" Brittany grinned. "Like the one on Mackinac Island in Michigan. You know. The white one with the porch that goes on and on and on. The big pillars. The beautiful grounds—"

Kurt asked, "Are you going to have a pool?"

Although several hotel owners had broached this topic before, there were no pools anywhere on the island and that's the status most residents preferred.

"Please," Lauren pleaded. "Please say you're going to have a pool."

"Yes," Brittany said, laughing. "A big pool. Heated. With hot tubs and waterfalls."

"Sweet!" Kurt exclaimed.

Sophie swallowed and took a deep breath. How could she be upset with someone so nice and perky?

"Awesome!" Lauren said.

"What's awesome?" Marty asked, tossing the bag of marshmallows between the kids and plopping into the lawn chair next to Brittany.

"You guys moving here!" Lauren shouted.

"A pool!" Kurt added.

Marty shot a look at Brittany.

Her excitement immediately fizzled. "Sorry," she said, cringing. "It slipped out."

Sophie attempted a smile, but one look at her and Marty's shoulders slumped. Brittany and the kids grew quiet.

"I'm sorry, Sophie," he said. "I meant to tell you myself. At the right time."

"It's okay, Brittany." Sophie reassured her soon-to-be sister-in-law. "There wasn't going to be a right time."

"Can we go for a walk?" Marty asked. "Talk?"

"Sure." She stood and crossed her arms, holding in the warmth.

As they walked along the beach, toward the forest, Sophie tried to find the positives in the situation. Marty would be back, Brittany was adorable, and they'd probably have children. Right next door, Sophie would have nieces and nephews and her kids would have cousins. The last thing she wanted to do was disappoint her brother only days before his wedding. "Marty—"

"Sophie, don't say anything," he said. "Not yet. Not until you've heard me out, okay?"

"This is going to take business away from the inn."

"That was my first concern," Marty acknowledged. "The truth is, Mirabelle has been steadily losing tourists for the last five years. If something isn't done to generate some interest in this island and to attract new visitors, Mirabelle's going to die a slow and painful death with or without a new hotel."

"None of the inns, hotels or B and Bs are at full capacity for the summer," she argued. "A new hotel will only make things worse."

"Soph, do you remember when we were kids most of the visitors to the island were families?"

She nodded.

"Well, lately the island's mainstay has become couples and weddings, but without a steady influx of families we can't survive."

"We're too quiet for families."

"Exactly. There isn't enough to do on the island. My hotel, with a pool, video-game rooms and a pizza parlor, will be a haven for families."

"No one else has a pool. You'll take business away from everyone."

"I can't take it away if it isn't there off the start," he said, sounding frustrated. "We can make it a community pool. I don't care. The golf course will make the biggest difference in bringing in more people."

"A golf course? Marty, how much land do you need for that?"

"The average course is about two hundred acres."

"That's half our forest!" She turned toward him, suddenly angry. "How can you just destroy it? Destroy everything Mom and Dad worked so hard to keep safe?"

"Something has to be done. Mirabelle is dying."

"Well, I have to be honest. I don't think your plan is going to help." She took comfort in knowing that the land was in a trust. "You have to get this approved by all of us, and I don't think—"

"Beth and Jackie have already said yes."

"What?" Her two sisters had already put their stamp of approval on Marty's project. This was too much.

"I only need your nod and we can go ahead with the plans."

"Well, you're not going to get it!" she said, charging away from him. "I won't let this happen!"

"Sophie! Stop. You said you'd listen before you make up your mind."

She spun around. "Even if I do give you the go-ahead, you'll still have to get everything approved by the town council before doing anything."

"I've scheduled a meeting with them for Tuesday night."

"While all this wedding stuff is going on?"

"Brittany's as excited as I am to get the ball rolling."

So soon. She didn't have a clue what to think, what to do, and there was no one on the island she could talk to, either. As a Rousseau, her opinion would likely influence others and, for Marty's sake, she didn't want to sway any opinions. The islanders needed to make up their own minds.

"Besides, this initial meeting should be a piece of cake,"

Marty continued, shrugging. "I'm just asking for approval to do a feasibility study. I'm an islander. Hometown boy makes good. They'll eat it up. But I need you behind me, otherwise it won't happen."

How could I get behind this?

"All I'm asking is that Tuesday night you listen to my presentation and think about it before you make up your mind. Okay?"

She debated. "All right. Fine. I'll wait to make up my mind. That doesn't mean I'm going to let you destroy trust land."

"This will be good for Mirabelle. I know it." He hugged her. "Will you come back to the fire?"

She shook her head.

"Don't be angry at me, Sophie."

"Then don't do this."

"I believe in it, Sophie. I love this island and I don't want to see it die." His smile was sad. "Come back to the fire. Please."

"You go. I need to walk some more." Thoroughly unsettled, Sophie set off down the beach.

FROM A DISTANCE, NOAH STARED at the fire. He'd been leaning against a large rock near the point for some time listening to the muted rumble of voices, hoping it would relax him and calm his thoughts. It had helped somewhat, but a part of him felt uneasy keeping separate from the group. Normally, he'd be in the thick of a party, joining in, talking and laughing. It wasn't like him to insulate himself from anything, but since the explosion, since losing his leg, it was as if he'd lost his footing in more ways than one.

He contented himself with watching Sophie, her smile in profile, the way the firelight illuminated her face and hair. The vision of her helped him block out the memories of the last fire he'd witnessed, the military truck burning after the explosion in Iraq. He'd struggled in the dirt, his foot hanging by a tangled mass of broken bone and torn skin, trying to get back to the burning vehicle. He'd passed out before help had arrived, the images of those flames seared in his memory.

This fire, though, was different, harmless, and Sophie looked beautiful in the periphery of light. He couldn't help noticing how none of her mannerisms had changed, and how he still remembered them after all these years. The way she curled one leg under her as she sat in the camp chair. Then she'd lean forward, an elbow on her knee, and rest her chin in her hand. Some of his fondest memories of Mirabelle had been sitting around a campfire with her. She'd always looked so beautiful in that flickering, golden light.

When she got up to talk with Marty, he could tell by the stiffness in her movements that something was wrong. She and Marty walked away from the fire. After a short time, she took off along the beach alone, moving fast. With a full moon lighting her way, even the steep rocky incline near the point didn't slow her progress.

Her head bent in concentration, her path would take her right past him. If he said nothing, she'd likely walk right by, none the wiser to his presence. He kept his mouth shut, held his breath. *Go by, Sophie. Go by.*

Suddenly, she stopped, looked up and put a hand to her chest as if he'd frightened her.

"Hey," he said. "It's just me."

"You scared me." She took a deep breath. "Why don't you go down by the fire? Marty would love to see you."

"Too many people."

She tilted her head at him. "But you love people."

"Not these days." He thought for a moment. "It's this…prosthesis business. Some people…"

"Treat you differently?"

He nodded.

"Have I ever…acted like that?"

"No. Except for when you didn't slap me my first day back on the island."

She chuckled.

"Some day all that awkwardness from others won't bother me at all. It's just not now."

Preoccupied, she gazed out at the water.

"Something happen with Marty?"

For a moment, she didn't say anything and then she opened her mouth and her news spewed out, like a geyser erupting into the air. Pacing beside him, barely catching her breath, she went on and on about how Marty wanted to build a hotel with pools and a golf course. Guessing she was too agitated to sit, Noah stood and walked toward the path in the woods. She followed, continuing to vent.

Even Noah understood the impact those changes would have on the face of this community. "Where's he planning on putting the hotel?"

"On the family trust land. After he's through, there won't be anything left of it," she said. "How can Marty and my sisters let this pristine forest go? I don't get it."

"He doesn't live here."

"Well, after he starts living here, he'll regret cutting down any part of these woods."

"So your sisters have already approved this?"

She nodded. "No one said anything to me." Soon, they left the forest behind, crossed Island Drive and walked along the dirt road that ran by the stables.

"Are *you* going to approve it?"

"Absolutely not. Other than the kids, this island is all I have. Destroy Mirabelle, and I've got nothing."

"Soph, that's not true. There's so much more to you than this island," he said, hoping to help her feel better. "All change isn't necessarily bad."

"A golf course? A pool? On Mirabelle? As we speak, my grandparents are rolling in their graves."

"What about the town council? Have they okayed it?"

"He's bringing the concept to them Tuesday night. Before getting contractors to the island to do a feasibility study, he wants to make sure the board will consider a proposal."

"So what are you going to do?"

"I don't know." She shook her head as if she were shaking a thought loose. "I don't want to talk about it anymore."

Amazing. She still had that uncanny ability to redirect herself, to shut down. The only time she'd ever done it with him had been when he'd been getting ready to leave the island. It had killed him that she wouldn't look at him, or face him.

That's when he'd basically kidnapped her and taken her to that hotel in Bayfield. He'd wanted to make her deal with him leaving, except in the end, he'd been the one who couldn't say goodbye and had left in the early morning hours while she was sound asleep. More than once he'd berated himself for being a coward, and the memories heightened his remorse.

"I'm sorry, Sophie," he said, on impulse.

"For what?"

"For not saying goodbye. For letting you wake up alone the morning I left." Before he knew it, they were back at his grandmother's house.

As if the memory of that morning was too much for her, she looked away, forced it back. "Thanks for listening tonight." She rubbed her arms as if she were chilled and took a deep breath.

"You cold?"

"A little."

"Do you want some tea?"

"Will that help you sleep?"

He laughed. "Nothing helps me sleep."

"Even medication?"

"The pills the doctors prescribed in the hospital worked for a while, but they also caused extreme nausea and made me tired all day long. I couldn't think straight."

They'd come to the house from the hillside, so Noah let them into the kitchen through the back door. He grabbed the teapot and filled it with water.

"Here," she said. "Let me do that. You go relax. Better yet, get ready for bed."

"Sophie—"

"I want you off my island, remember?"

"Yeah, I remember." Suddenly he did feel incredibly tired. The past few days of activity, quite possibly, were doing the job. "You don't—"

"Humor me." She skirted past him and put the teapot on the stove.

It irritated him that she could move so much faster than him, zipping this way and that. He wanted to grab her and slow her down. Before he'd made it to the steps, she was bent over emptying out the dishwasher. *Damn.* Sophie had filled out beautifully. The skinny teenager had been replaced by a curvy woman with flared hips and full breasts. Dwelling on what she'd feel like was definitely not going to help him sleep.

He tore his gaze away, climbed the steps and traded jeans for flannel pajama pants. As he brushed his teeth and washed his face, the sound of Sophie now loading the dishwasher filtered up from downstairs. He had to admit it was comforting having someone else in the house.

He emerged from the bathroom, minus his leg, to find she'd snuck upstairs while he'd had the water running in the bathroom. His bedcovers were turned down, and the windows were slightly open, allowing for a gentle cross breeze. The stage was set. The only thing missing was a woman. How long had it been? Too long. Sophie would be just what one of his doctors had ordered.

Bad, bad idea. He lay on his side, scrunched up the pillow and drew the blanket over him. For the first time in a long while, he wasn't dreading the night.

Soft footsteps sounded in the hall. He opened his suddenly heavy eyes to see Sophie tiptoeing toward him. "I straightened up downstairs and made you some herbal tea." She quietly set a steaming mug of chamomile on his bedside table, next to his Beretta. "Why do you have this gun here?"

"It helps me feel safe."

"You are safe. You should put it away."

He grabbed the gun and slid it under his pillow. "Not yet." He closed his eyes. "'Night, Soph."

"Good night." She hesitated and then whispered, "I won't be back tomorrow."

No. She'd be back in his dreams.

In the shadowy hallway, Sophie stood quietly outside the door to Noah's bedroom and listened to the sound of his steady breathing. He looked warm and comfortable and she was now chilly in the night air. A war waged inside her, and it took every ounce of resistance she could muster to not sneak along his backside and wrap her arms around him.

What in the world had come over her? She had wanted him off her island. Honestly. Truly. But tonight something had changed. Tonight, as they'd walked and talked, for the first time since he'd been back, Sophie had caught a glimpse of the old Noah, the Noah whom she'd always loved.

She wanted to feel *that* Noah's arms cinched tightly around her, his hands caressing her skin. Her body ached to feel that again.

Only *her* Noah had broken her heart. And that heart had never healed. *Her* Noah had left once. He'd leave again. She, on the other hand, had children who needed a stable home. As the oldest Rousseau, she had duties and responsibilities. While many things had changed through the years, one constant remained. Sophie could no more leave Mirabelle today than she could have fifteen years ago.

CHAPTER NINE

"TEN...ELEVEN...TWE...LVE."

Unable to force out another pull-up, Noah dropped down from the bar he'd installed within the laundry room doorframe. He'd already done as many sit-ups and push-ups as he could manage and, in as sorry a shape as he was in, he'd done enough for the night. It was hard to believe that once upon a time he'd actually kept up the workout regiment of the soldiers to whom he'd been assigned.

He glanced at the clock. Ten minutes to seven. Tuesday night's council meeting would soon be starting. All day, while he'd been scraping and painting the house, he hadn't seen hide nor hair of Sophie. She had to feel stuck between a rock and a hard place, caught as she was between wanting to help out her brother and wanting to keep Mirabelle undamaged and unchanged.

"Ah, hell." His bum leg would make him a little late, but for some crazy reason he needed to be at that council meeting.

Fifteen minutes later, Noah stood in the foyer of the town hall, listening to some minor business about garbage pickups. He debated whether or not he should actually go inside. He could stand in the foyer and listen to the debate, or he could do what he'd intended and head right toward Sophie so she'd know he was there for her. There was only one problem. What made him think she'd care? She might not. Strangely enough, he did.

Noah stepped into the room. With its indoor-outdoor carpeting, fluorescent lights, painted concrete walls and the smell of industrialized sanitizer permeating the air, he felt as if he was back in elementary school.

The council members, including Noah's dad, sat at a long table at the front of the room. They looked up when he came in and Carl Andersen, owner of the Rock Point Lodge and an old classmate of Noah's, stopped talking. The entire room turned to see what had captured Carl's attention. *Great.* A grand entrance was not what he'd intended.

Sophie sat toward the front next to Marty. Noah walked down the side aisle and sat in the empty seat by her side. Ignoring the rest of the room, he whispered, "I hope it's okay that I came."

She gave him a funny little half smile. "It's fine."

Noah's dad cleared his throat. "Let's move on, Carl."

"Oh, yeah," Carl said, looking at the papers in front of him. "Where was I?"

After an introduction, Marty walked toward the front of the room with a large portfolio in his hand. He grabbed the microphone and said, "Everyone's going to have their own opinion about what I have to say. Some of you are going to love the idea and some of you are going to hate it. All I ask is that you give the possibility fair consideration." He paused and looked out over the crowd. "I want to build a new hotel."

That met with a few comments.

"We don't need more rooms."

"You're moving back to the island?"

"About time."

"I know the island already has excess occupancy, but I've got a plan to attract more people." Marty outlined his proposal. "I want to have two pools and I have plans for a municipal golf course that everyone in this room should be interested in."

His comment was met with stunned silence. Noah looked around. If Marty had been an outsider, they would've given him a quick and loud piece of their minds, but because he was one of their own, they politely kept their opinions to themselves. For the moment. When Marty finished summarizing his proposal, the resulting response was a combination of eagerness and outrage.

"Okay, okay," Carl said, quieting the room. "I don't think Marty's finished yet."

Marty set down the mike and looked out at the group. "Before you all get dead set against the idea, here are the facts. In the past five years, all of you have spent more and more money on promotion, and every year your sales have been slipping. The number of tourists visiting this island has been steadily dropping every year for the past five years."

"How do you know that?" Bob Henderson, the owner of the drugstore asked.

"The ferry company shared passenger figures."

"You think two pools and a golf course are the answers?"

"I think it will draw more families with kids."

"Maybe we like things the way they are," someone yelled.

"Look," Marty said. "I'm not talking about building a huge, all-inclusive type resort here. Everyone benefits from this venture. My guests would visit your businesses, and the golf course would be municipal. We'd all benefit from that."

The arguing went on and on, back and forth. Marty's proposal threatened to tear the island in two.

"I'm not asking for anyone to approve my plans tonight," Marty practically yelled. "All I'm looking for is approval to do a feasibility study. To bring engineers and contractors onto the island to determine whether or not a golf course and pool are even possible. Once we find out if it's even possible, then I'll be back looking for approval to get formal bids."

"Okay." Carl quieted everyone. "Is there anyone in this room who thinks this is a good idea?"

One hand raised, then another. Marty, no doubt, had what he was looking for, a crack in the stoic foundation. During a moment of silence, Noah's dad said, "Sophie. What do you think?"

Marty's gaze spun toward his sister. She could make or break this for him. "Be honest," he whispered. "But please don't kill it right away."

"I think," Sophie said, "that while I'm personally dead set against this—" she glanced at Marty "—it never hurts to consider possibilities. Marty knows what this island means to all of us. If there's anyone who can do this while preserving Mirabelle's integrity it's one of our own."

After more mumbling and arguing, the council called for a vote. All council members except Noah's dad were in favor of allowing Marty to go ahead with gathering whatever information he needed to fully develop a final proposal, but in the end Marty would need a unanimous vote to implement his plan.

The meeting ended and people either left or milled about. Sophie stood. "I'm surprised to see you here, Noah."

"Hey, I had to give the town something to talk about aside from Marty's deal."

Carrying his portfolio, Marty came down the aisle. "Thanks for coming, Noah."

"No problem."

"After all this," Sophie said to Marty, "you still up for movie night with all the nieces and nephews?"

"Brittany and I wouldn't miss it for the world."

Noah's dad came toward them. "No hard feelings, Marty, right?"

"Not at all, Jim. This is your home. You gotta trust your gut."

"Noah, you want to go get something to eat?"

The offer surprised Noah, until he realized his dad's motivation probably had more to do with trying to keep Noah away from Sophie than anything else. "I'm not really hungry right now, Dad. Thanks."

"Suit yourself."

Some islanders came up to Marty to get more details on his proposal, and Noah and Sophie found themselves alone.

"Sophie!" said a woman near the doors.

With her plump cheeks and ready smile, the woman looked familiar to Noah. "Is that Lynn Duffy?" Noah whispered.

"Mmm-hmm."

It was the hair that had thrown him. Her long wavy locks had changed from solid black to completely white since Noah had last seen her. "Hello, Mrs. Duffy."

She nodded at him. "Sophie, you want to join us for a beer at the pub?"

"No, thanks, Lynn. Some other night."

Lynn glanced at Noah and frowned. "Well…okay."

After she'd left, Noah whispered, "I'm sensing they don't want us together."

"Ya think?"

They stepped outside and by unspoken agreement headed toward Noah's house. Suddenly, Sophie laughed.

"What's so funny?"

"You. Calling everyone mister and missus. Do you know any of the adults' first names?"

"No." He chuckled. "Hey. I was eighteen when I left here. Gimme a break. It was always Mrs. Duffy, Mr. Setterberg, yada yada. I'm surprised my dad didn't make me call him Chief Bennett."

They walked along in silence for another block or so, neither seeming to know what to say. Something he couldn't identify had changed between them since last night.

"You look like you got some sun today," she said, clearly uncomfortable.

"Did some more painting."

They reached Noah's street and turned up the hill. "Did you sleep last night?" she asked.

"Four hours. Your magic did the trick last night. What're you doing tonight, tomorrow night, the night after that?" he said, chuckling.

"I did some research on the Internet about that mirror therapy you mentioned yesterday. Have you ever tried it?" she asked.

"Once or twice," he said, hesitating. He looked away, out toward the lake. The exercise had a funny way of making him miss his foot even more.

"The studies indicate it can make a difference after a short while—"

"Stop," he said, cutting her off. "Don't psychoanalyze me. And *don't* doubt that I want off this island as much as you want me gone."

She fell silent.

"Look, I'm sorry. I'm doing the best I can." They'd reached Grandma Bennett's house. "You should get back to your kids," he said.

"Are you kidding me? Home is the last place I want to be," she said. "Marty and Brittany are having a sleepover in my apartment with all the nieces and nephews."

That actually sounded like fun. Maybe some day he'd have that kind of comfortable relationship with Kurt and Lauren.

"We need to get you sleeping through the night," she said. "The tea helped last night, didn't it?"

He nodded and climbed the porch steps.

"Let's give that another shot."

Too tired to argue, he went upstairs as she headed into the kitchen to make tea. After washing up and brushing his teeth, he went into his bedroom, traded jeans for flannel pants and pulled off his shirt. He was searching through the dresser for a warm shirt—the nights were often chilly even in June—when the sound of footsteps came from the hall.

"Here's some tea." Carrying two cups, Sophie came through the door. On seeing him naked from the waist up, she stopped.

He tensed, self-conscious about his body for the first time in his life. Other than the nurses in the hospital, no woman had seen the damage done to him over the years.

The moon cut a swath across her neck and chest, but he couldn't see her face, couldn't read her eyes. "All those scars," she whispered. "You look like a soldier."

Hardly. He'd done what he could for people in need whose paths he'd crossed through the years, often doing more than fighting their battles with his articles and books, but it wasn't the same. He turned away.

"Oh, Noah. Your back, too." Shrapnel from the Iraqi explosion had hit his stomach and chest, but his back had been virtually shredded, taking the brunt of the punishment. She set his cup of tea on the bedside table and sat down in a nearby chair. "You must've been a bloody mass of pulp."

She had that right. Quickly, he pulled the first shirt he could find over his head. "Yeah. I had to be on my stomach for several weeks in the hospital." Sitting on the edge of the bed, he took off the prosthetic.

Having her so near physically, in this intimate setting, was getting to him. He might not be himself, but he was still a man, and Sophie was…well, Sophie. The only woman he'd ever loved. The two of them alone here, at night, was not a smart idea. That's when he realized what had changed. Walking and talking last night had dispelled the anger between them.

"Sophie—"

"I'll go in a minute."

He had to admit falling asleep with her nearby sounded comforting, and as long as she stayed in that chair and didn't touch him, he'd be okay. He fell onto his stomach on top of the light blanket and stretched out.

"Will you be able to sleep?"

"Probably." Already his eyelids felt heavy. "A back rub sounds nice." Had he actually said that aloud?

Sure enough the mattress gave way as Sophie sat next to him. Her hands were on his shoulders massaging and kneading. Down his spine, working out the knots. Then her hands were all over him, harder now, massaging, bringing relief. He understood why he needed her, but Sophie? "Remind me again why you're doing this," he whispered.

"I told you. I want you off my island."

"Liar."

Her touch softened, and before he knew what was happening, he drifted off in a deep sleep. When he opened his eyes, it was dark outside. The room was chilly, telling him he'd slept for hours. With the next breath he became aware of a warm body snuggled behind him. Sophie's arm was over his back, wrapped around his side, and a feeling of contentedness rolled over him in a slow, quiet wave.

He shifted, pulled a nearby blanket over them and turned onto his back. Sound asleep, she made a soft sound as she cuddled against his side. His arm had no place to go except around her. "You're playing with fire staying here," he whispered into the chilly night air.

"I don't care," she murmured, still half-asleep. "I missed you."

"I've missed you, too." He had, more than he'd let himself believe. As he closed his eyes and drifted off once again, he couldn't shake the feeling that safe wasn't being on Mirabelle. Safe was being in Sophie's arms.

SOPHIE CAME AWAKE TO THE QUIET, lonesome call of a mourning dove. With the colors of predawn tinting the room in pale, pink light, she became fully aware of having fallen asleep in Noah's bed and having slept there the entire night. He'd slept, too, but at what cost?

Last night something had come over her, suddenly, completely, uncontrollably. She'd seen his scars, imagined the pain he'd gone through and the urge to comfort him had overwhelmed her. As if she'd walked through a time warp, she'd gone back to square one with Noah. Just like that.

You are so asking for a twice-broken heart.

Though she didn't remember either of them waking, he'd turned in the middle of the night and drawn covers over them. He was behind her now, keeping her warm, his steady breath skimming her neck, his arm tucked around her, his body so close along the full length of her backside she couldn't move without sliding her skin against his.

A raging awareness of her body—and Noah's—sprang to life inside her. Every bone, every muscle, every inch of her skin was tuned to Noah. If only she could strip off her clothes and feel him, his warmth, next to her.

Isaac had never liked making love in the morning, and yet the few times she and Noah had managed to spend all night together, their sunrise lovemaking had been some of their more tender moments together. Slow and warm, Noah had never been in a hurry.

Oh, God, Isaac. I'm so sorry.

She'd been a lukewarm wife for him. Oh, she'd been kind, respectful, considerate and, in a way, loving. They'd enjoyed each other's company. She'd been content with his lovemaking and, as far as she knew, she'd pleased him, but never once in all the years she'd been with Isaac had she felt this kind of consuming arousal. The kind that drove a woman to do crazy things. The kind that if she didn't leave right now…

Leave. Now. Before he wakes up.

But I want this.

What about Lauren and Kurt?

You may have learned to live with not knowing for certain whether Noah or Isaac is Kurt and Lauren's biological father, but Noah won't accept that. He'll want to know.

That worked like a splash of frigid water to her face. Carefully, she lifted Noah's arm and inched away from him. She glanced back at his still form as she tiptoed out the door. He'd better get well quick and leave Mirabelle, or she was going to find herself in deep trouble. There was no promise here, no future, only the messy past.

On entering her home, she found Marty asleep on the couch with Brittany and all their nieces and nephews crashed on the floor. Marty cracked open his eyes when she walked into the room.

"Thanks for staying," she whispered.

"Where were you?" he asked, still bleary-eyed.

Kurt groaned and rolled over in his sleeping bag on the floor in the family room. Sophie watched him for a moment, making sure he wasn't awake.

"Were you at Noah's?" Marty asked.

"Shh," Sophie said and motioned they take their conversation into the kitchen.

Marty followed her, the look on his face neither accusatory nor judgmental, only concerned. "You slept at Noah's?"

"It was an accident," she whispered. "I know what you're going to say. Don't. Nothing happened."

"Yet." He shook his head. "Sophie, Noah's never lied to you." He was struggling to keep his voice down. "He's never given you reason for false hope. There's no happy ending to this story."

"I know, Marty." Better than anyone.

NOAH ROLLED OVER IN BED only to have the glare of a midmorning sun smack him in the face. Groggy as hell, he flopped back to his other side and pried open his eyes. He felt like death warmed over. What was the matter with him?

Then he saw the dent from Sophie's head on the pillow and the previous night came back to him. He'd slept, that's what'd happened, damned close to a full eight-hour stretch.

He tucked her pillow in front of him, smelled her lingering scent on the linens, like a fresh breeze over open water, and fell back asleep to the remembered feeling of her hands all over him. Isaac had been one lucky son of a bitch.

CHAPTER TEN

ADD A FULL NIGHT'S SLEEP on top of all the work he'd been doing on the house these past several days, and Noah's appetite was back with a vengeance. He devoured a plate full of fried eggs, Canadian bacon, hash browns and toast and then went outside to finish painting and scraping the rest of the house. He was crouched on his knees on the porch, putting a coat of paint on the railing when Marty came up the walk.

"Hey." Noah dipped his brush in the paint can and finished off the last spindle. "What's up?"

"Word got around you still hold the island record for consecutive table tennis championships," Marty said in a relative monotone, his mouth set in a stern line. "We're having a tournament this morning."

Noah pushed himself upright and stepped away from the railing. "That's not why you came up here."

Marty hesitated and then stomped onto the porch. "What are you doing, Noah?"

Right. This was about Sophie. Last night. Noah would be damned before he'd defend himself, but he didn't want to give the wrong impression, either. "We fell asleep. That's it."

"I'm supposed to believe she spent the entire night here and nothing happened?"

"That's right."

"Well, I'm going to bet you wanted something to happen. A lot of something."

That, Noah couldn't argue.

"Does that mean you're thinking of staying on Mirabelle?"

"No." Noah shook his head. Just the thought of an isolated winter on this island sent an uneasy chill up his spine.

Marty paced the length of the porch. "I know what it feels like to want off this island. I couldn't wait to head off to college. Now I can't wait to move back here, raise a family, run my own business. People change, Noah."

"Not this people."

"So there's no way you're staying?"

"No."

"Does she know that?"

"Yes."

"Do you still love her?"

"Hell, Marty, how should I know?" Now it was Noah's turn to pace, albeit with a bit of a limp.

"Then I get back to the original question. What the hell are you doing?"

"Obviously, I don't know."

"Well, do everyone a favor and figure it out before hearts get broken all over again." Marty went back to the steps.

A surge of protectiveness toward Sophie welled inside Noah. "What about you?"

"What do you mean?"

"Wanting to tear down Rousseau forest land to build a brand-new hotel, pools and a golf course?" Noah couldn't believe he cared one way or the other. "Talk about breaking hearts. How can you do that to Sophie?"

"You don't live on this island anymore, so you don't understand the situation."

"You're threatening to destroy tradition, history. That's pretty simple."

"This island is dying, Noah, and all the residents refuse to see it. Since you don't live here anymore and never plan to live here again, maybe you should stay out of it." Marty pounded down the porch steps. "In the meantime, there are a couple of kids at the inn dying to beat you in table tennis."

"You still want me to come down?"

"I'm not going to figure this one out for Sophie. Unlike the rest of this island. She's a grown woman. She can take care of herself." Once in the yard, he turned. "Do you want to play Ping-Pong or not?"

Noah's initial reaction was not. All those people, the activity, the conversation, the looks. Kids staring at him, he didn't mind. They were curious. What bothered him most was the way adults often studied him, noticing his gait and then their gazes shifting away. These days, insulating himself felt more comfortable. He didn't have to watch everyone else getting on with his or her life while his stagnated.

"Noah, man, you're not a hermit." Marty's voice broke through Noah's thoughts. "It's not your way."

No. It wasn't.

"Maybe you're not up for the competition," Marty challenged with a sudden gleam in his eye. "Maybe you've gotten soft."

Noah laughed. "All right, Little Mart. You're on."

SOPHIE TOOK HER MIND OFF last night's town council meeting, not to mention what had happened between her and Noah, and locked herself in her office Wednesday morning to catch up on some work. It felt good to push everything out of her mind and focus, if only for a few hours. After lunch, she rejoined the wedding party outside and was surprised to find Marty playing against Noah in the deciding match of a table tennis tournament.

"Game point." Marty chuckled. It was his serve. "Get ready to lose, Noah."

"Go, Uncle Marty!" Sophie's nieces and nephews cheered for their uncle.

"Noah! Noah! Noah!" Lauren chanted.

"You're dead meat, Noah," Kurt yelled. "You can do it, Uncle Marty!"

Sophie glanced up at her son. There was something decidedly less than good-natured in his support of Marty. What was that all about?

While it was disconcerting having Noah in such close proximity to Lauren and Kurt, it was good to see Noah laughing and interacting with Marty and Brittany's wedding guests. His skin had color back and he was already gaining some weight. He grinned and Sophie saw a glimmer of a new Noah, an all grown-up and mature, full-fledged man. A man who could take care of himself. Not long now and he'd be leaving to get on with his life. Good. That was good.

"Here we go!" Marty served, and Noah returned. They volleyed back and forth. Marty slammed a fast one and Noah returned a little too hard. The ball missed the table by no more than a quarter of an inch. "Yes!" Marty raised his arms in victory as the crowd that had gathered clapped and cheered. "Finally, I beat you at something."

"Good game, Uncle Marty." Kurt tapped his fist against Marty's in midair.

"You did your best," Lauren said, patting Noah on the back.

"Maybe I let him win." A grin on his face, Noah set down his paddle.

"Yeah, right." Kurt rolled his eyes and turned to walk away.

"Hey," Sophie whispered to him, setting a hand on his shoulder. "What's going on?"

"Nothing." He shrugged her off and walked away.

When she turned back around the crowd had dispersed, leaving only Sophie, Lauren and Noah.

"Glad to see you made it down here," she said.

"Marty came up to the house and challenged me to a game. What could I do? Besides, I needed a break from painting."

"They're setting up teams for a boccie ball tournament," Lauren said. "Will you be on my team, Noah?"

"I don't know, sweetie."

"Oh, come on!" She dragged him across the lawn toward the sign-up table Jan was manning.

"Noah, do you remember Jan?" Sophie asked.

Jan looked up briefly, scowled and then went back to her paperwork.

"Sure, I remember. Your husband runs the equipment rental place, right?"

When Jan only nodded, Sophie said, "Yep, that's Ron."

"Noah's going to sign up on my boccie ball team," Lauren announced.

"Wait a minute," Noah interrupted.

"All the teams are full," Jan said.

"I thought I needed three more people," Lauren complained.

"We had to shuffle things around to make the teams more even."

Sophie cocked her head at Jan. Something about that excuse smelled fishy, but the less time Noah spent around Lauren, the better.

"Since when?" Lauren asked.

"Since you were watching the Ping-Pong tournament."

"What—"

"It's okay," Noah said, patting Lauren's shoulder. "I need to get some more work done, anyway."

"Oh, all right," Lauren said, disappointed.

They walked away from Jan's sign-up table and were heading toward the beach when one of Lauren's cousins yelled, "Lauren! It's your turn for karaoke."

"Coming!" She ran toward the inn. "See you guys later."

That left Sophie alone with Noah. "How are you feeling?" she asked.

"Good. I slept…really well last night," he said, then quickly changed the subject. "Went into town first thing and picked up some groceries. I actually rented a bike."

"How did pedaling go?"

"I did okay." By this time they'd wandered to the water's edge. Noah picked up a rock and skipped it over the surface of the water. "This place isn't as friendly as I remembered."

"Why do you say that?"

"Little things here and there. Old man Newman was at the grocery store along with his son. He barely looked up from the shelf he was stocking. His son was downright rude."

"Mike Newman rude?"

"Feels like a conspiracy to me." Noah grinned. "I think they want me off this island. Probably more than you do." He kicked the toe of his tennis shoe into the sand. "Can't blame them, I guess. I've never disguised the fact that I hated living here. Not to mention I pretty much put my dad through hell when I was a teenager. Then there's always you—"

"Sophie!" The shout came from behind them. Josie was coming toward them. "We need your help. Brittany's having a bit of a meltdown."

"About what?"